"I'm not tell-ing you this to upset you,"

Josh said. "I just don't want you to be disappointed in case your father turns out to be a flake after all."

A deep furrow appeared between Winnie's eyes. "I can't believe you!" she shouted. "You're the one who bulldozed me into trusting him in the first place! Make up your mind."

"I'm not saying I've changed my whole perception of him. He could still be a terrific guy. I'm just saying we should be open-minded."

Winnie nodded knowingly. "This isn't really about my father is it?" she said. "You're just jealous! You're jealous that my father stole your thunder at your stupid exhibit tonight. You're jealous that he has a way of talking to people that makes them feel special."

"My stupid exhibit?!" Josh thundered. "Oh, that's real supportive. My exhibit isn't any stupider than your stupid benefit!"

"Oh," Winnie cried, stamping her foot on the floor. "So now my father's a sleaze, and my benefit's stupid? Well, if you think it's so stupid, you can just skip it. Believe me, you won't be missed!"

Don't miss these books
in the exciting FRESHMAN DORM series

And, coming soon . . .

FRESHMAN RIVALS

LINDA A. COONEY

HarperPaperbacks
A Division of HarperCollinsPublishers

This is a work of fiction. The characters, incidents, and dialogues are products of the author's imagination and are not to be construed as real. Any resemblance to actual events or persons, living or dead, is entirely coincidental.

HarperPaperbacks *A Division of* HarperCollins*Publishers*
10 East 53rd Street, New York, N.Y. 10022

Cover art by Tony Greco

First printing: August 1991

Printed in the United States of America

HarperPaperbacks and colophon are trademarks of HarperCollins*Publishers*

10 9 8 7 6 5 4 3 2 1

One

··················

"Manic depressive," Winnie Gottlieb read out loud from her psychology textbook. She lay on the floor of her dorm room, her head pillowed against a rolled-up, oversized Mickey Mouse sweatshirt. Her feet, warm and cozy in fuzzy, tiger-striped socks, were propped up on her unmade bed. "A psychosis characterized by alternating periods of mania; excessive, persistent enthusiasm; and melancholia or mental depression," she continued. "Sound familiar?"

Melissa McDormand, Winnie's roommate, gave no answer. She was sprawled on her bed, her head buried in her chemistry notes. Her red hair was pulled up in its usual ponytail, and her freckled face was wrinkled in concentration. Sitting at Melissa's desk was her boyfriend, Brooks Baldwin. His blond curls shook as he turned his head back and forth from his scribbled notes on the desk to the white sheet of paper rapidly filling with black type in the typewriter.

"Okay, I'll give you a hint," Winnie babbled, even though no one was listening. "It sounds like *me!* Or, at least, I *used* to act manic-depressive, don't you think? Why else would I have had such high highs and such low lows? Not that I had a clinical case or anything, but it makes you realize what a fine line there is between mental illness and normal behavior. We're all on a spectrum, really. But at least now I realize I'm just a very enthusiastic person with normal mood swings. Anyway, lately I've been feeling a lot more mellow. Haven't you two noticed that?"

Melissa sighed as she raised her head from her spiral notebook. "Winnie?" she asked politely. "Do you think you could become even more mellow and read to yourself? I've got a chemistry quiz tomorrow, and I'd really like to get my studying done so I can get to sleep by ten. I've got track practice tomorrow at 7:00 A.M."

"Sorry," Winnie said, wiggling her feet. She let her textbook rest on her chest and gazed up at the fishnetting on the wall above her bed. The netting held all her essentials: paperback novels, incense, shiny, lycra tights in every color of the rainbow, and mini-bags of Nacho Cheese Doritos, just in case she got a craving in the middle of the night and didn't want to walk all the way to her closet, where she'd stashed a few Half-Pounder bags.

Winnie felt safe and secure, surrounded by all her familiar belongings and close friends. But the good feeling didn't just come from the outside. For the first time since she'd come to the University of Springfield, Winnie felt stable, really stable, on the inside. She was studying hard in all her classes, and had found a focus for her scattered energy by volunteering at the Crisis Hotline. Best of all, she'd finally gotten back together with her boyfriend, Josh Gaffey. They'd suffered through many fights and break-ups over the last months, but things were finally on an even keel.

Thump! Thump! Thump! It sounded like something heavy and metallic was pushing against Winnie's door.

"Did you hear that?" Winnie asked Brooks and Melissa, who'd looked up from their studies.

"Open the door. Open the door. Open the door," repeated a high-pitched, nasal voice outside in the hall.

"Sounds like a deranged Munchkin," Winnie

said, rising to her feet at the same time Melissa did. "I'm almost afraid to see who it is."

"Stand back," Brooks said, jumping out of his chair and beating Winnie to the door. "Melissa, stay where you are. You don't know who's behind there."

"I'm sure it's nothing to worry about," Winnie said, amused at how protective Brooks was. "At the worst, it's a drunken jock about to spill a bucket of Jell-O all over the floor."

Slowly, cautiously, Brooks opened the door a crack. "I don't see anything," he said, looking out. He opened the door wider.

"Winnie! Winnie! I must find Winnie!" said the high-pitched nasal voice. Winnie looked down. The voice was coming from a three-foot high, molded plastic, neon green robot. The robot was almost as wide as it was tall, with a black, hollow sphere on top that seemed to be its head. Inside the sphere, an infrared beam went on and off like a winking eye.

"What is that?!" Melissa exclaimed, her brown eyes wide.

"I am Alphie!" the robot answered, voice emanating from deep inside its chest. "And I must find Winnie."

"Take me to your leader," Brooks joked, stepping back as the robot wheeled into the room.

"I'm Winnie," Winnie said, laughing.

At the sound of her voice, Alphie began to spin around, and colorful Christmas lights along the sides of his body flashed on and off. "Winnie! Winnie!" it said deliriously, careening toward her. It stopped just inches from her tiger-striped feet and extended its mechanical arms. A grocery bag hung over one arm; the other offered a folded piece of paper.

"Are these for me?" Winnie asked, gently unhooking the grocery bag and taking the piece of paper.

"Sweets for the sweet," Alphie answered, lights still flashing.

Winnie looked inside the grocery bag and laughed again. It was filled with her favorite junk food: Hostess chocolate cupcakes, Entenmann's chocolate chip cookies, and, of course, a bag of Nacho Cheese Doritos. Then she unfolded the piece of paper. It was a flyer, announcing the upcoming U. of S. Computer Fair.

"Thanks, Alphie," Winnie said. "Is there anything else?"

"Yes," the robot said. A door opened in its stomach, and a red rose fell out. "I love you."

"Uh oh . . ." Brooks said, giving Winnie a grin. "It looks like Josh has a little competition." He went back to Melissa's desk and sat down at the typewriter.

"I have a feeling Josh is behind all this," Melissa said, getting comfortable on her bed again.

Winnie knelt by Alphie and picked up the rose. "He's so cute!"

"Talking about me?" Josh Gaffey asked, as he appeared in the open doorway. His brown hair fell across his forehead, and he wore a rumpled T-shirt over ripped jeans. There was a hole in the toe of one of his scuffed, leather moccasins.

"Of course we're not talking about you," Winnie said, putting her arm around the robot. "We're talking about my new boyfriend."

Josh tried to look shocked, but his eyes gleamed mischievously. "I don't know what you see in him," he said. "He's too short for you."

Winnie opened and closed the door in Alphie's stomach and manipulated the multi-jointed arms. "Did you really invent this, Josh?"

"I hope so." Josh stifled a yawn. "I've been up every night for the past two weeks, programming him for the computer fair."

"Is it a contest?" Winnie asked, holding the rose up to her nose and inhaling its perfume.

"No," Josh said, coming into the room and sitting on the floor by his creation. "It's more of an exhibition of new technology. A lot of big computer manufacturers come to show their latest models, and students show off their inventions, hoping to get someone interested in marketing them. I'm still not quite sure how to market Alphie, though." Josh patted Alphie's shiny black globe of a head.

"He's certainly a good delivery boy," Winnie said, tearing open the bag of Doritos. "Maybe grocery stores could make a bigger model and use it to deliver groceries to people who don't have cars."

"I don't know," Josh said doubtfully, as he wrapped his arms around Winnie. "Even if we told Alphie where these other people live, he'd keep coming back here to room 152 in Forest Hall. I guess he takes after his creator." Josh gave Winnie a squeeze and planted feathery kisses all over her face. Winnie wanted to cry, she was so happy. After months of having an on-again, off-again relationship, it felt so good to be in Josh's arms.

"Too bad you can't program Alphie to write my paper for me," Brooks said, trying to find his place in his notes so he could resume typing.

"Not to be a party pooper," Melissa said, "but since Alphie can't do our studying for us, maybe we'd better get back to work."

"Lighten up!" Alphie said in his nasal voice. Everybody laughed, including Melissa.

"Okay, okay, I can take a hint," Melissa said, shutting her notebook. "Maybe we all deserve a little study break."

"I know I do," Brooks said, dropping down to

the floor from his chair and reaching for the box of chocolate chip cookies. "I've been working on this paper for the past three days. Thank goodness, it's just about done.

"How is honors college?" Josh asked Brooks. "I hear you have to write a ten-page paper every week."

"You heard right," Brooks said. "It's tough, but it's good discipline. At this point, I can knock out a paper twice as fast as I used to."

"He's getting good grades, too," Melissa said proudly.

"How about you?" Brooks said, pulling Melissa down onto the floor beside him and tackling her with a hug. "This girl's pre-med, *and* she runs track, *and* she's pulling close to a 4.0 average."

"Excuse me, excuse me!" Melissa said, struggling to raise her hand even though Brooks had draped his sturdy body across her. "As long as we're bragging about people we know, I'd like to mention that my roommate, Winnifred Lynn Gottlieb, is not only doing well in all her classes and working at the Crisis Hotline, but she's also singlehandedly organizing a benefit to remodel the hotline's office which, by the way, could really use it. Have you seen it? It's drab, drab, drab."

"That's so true," Winnie said. "Just answering the phones there for a few hours can make you depressed enough to want to call the hotline yourself."

"Sounds like we could all use a break from our everyday routines," Brooks said, feeding Melissa a soft, round cookie.

"I definitely need to clear out my brain," Josh agreed. "Right now it's embedded with software commands."

"I've got it," Brooks said, sitting up. "I know what we can do—whitewater rafting!"

"What?" Melissa asked, lying on her back on the floor, looking up at him.

"My dorm is sponsoring a whitewater rafting trip down the Wahalla River, a week from Saturday," Brooks explained. "I think we should all go."

"You've got to be kidding," Winnie said, huddling inside Josh's protective embrace. "Whitewater rafting? I've heard that's really dangerous!"

"Me, too," Melissa said. "I read in the paper last year about some executives from a big company who went whitewater rafting. Their boat hit a rock and two of them drowned."

"That was a fluke," Brooks said, "Those guys were doing a Class Five whitewater without a guide or the proper equipment. The Wahalla's Class Four at the most, and they give you helmets and life preservers and everything. I've done it loads of times. It's incredibly exciting!"

Winnie tried to imagine herself being tossed about by the wild waves. At one time, she might have found the idea exciting, just one more way to push life to the extreme. But now, all she could picture was her head hitting a rock and her body being pulled under the water, whirling and spinning as she was sucked into oblivion. Winnie shivered with fear. She didn't want to take any unnecessary risks.

"I wish I could go," Winnie said, feeling a little guilty for being such a scaredy cat, "but the trip is the same day as the benefit for the hotline. And since I've made a commitment to help raise money, I can't back out of it."

"We'll be back by sundown," Brooks promised. "What time's your benefit?"

"Eight o'clock," Winnie said. "But I have to be there all day to set up. You guys should go, though."

"I don't know," Josh said, "it sounds like fun, but if you're not going to go . . ."

"Look," Winnie said, playing with a strand of his soft, silky hair, "you're not going to see me all day anyway since I'll be so busy. You might as well go and have a good time."

"Count me out," Melissa said. "I can't afford to take a whole day off."

"Why not?" Brooks asked. "Do you have a big test coming up?"

"Well, no."

"A paper, a special project?"

Melissa gave a small smile. "No."

"Chicken, perhaps?" Brooks asked, slipping a hand under her gray U. of S. sweatshirt to tickle her bare stomach.

"No! No!" Melissa shouted, giggling helplessly.

"Then what's your problem?" Brooks blew raspberries against her neck as he tickled her.

"Okay! Okay!" Melissa yelped. "You talked me into it!"

"So that makes three of us," Brooks said.

"Just promise me one thing," Winnie implored Josh. "Promise you'll be careful. I don't want anything to happen to you."

"I'm sure it's perfectly safe," Josh said. "Besides, what happened to your sense of adventure?"

"It's been tamed," Winnie said. "And I like it that way."

In the morning, Winnie jogged easily through the streets of downtown Springfield, her compact legs pumping evenly in their black lace tights. Over the tights, she wore black running shorts, and a hot pink stretch top that showed off her strong, rounded, upper body. Her dangling Fred and

Wilma Flintstone earrings jiggled on either side of her bare neck.

As she ran down the Strand, an elegant street of brownstones with boutiques, cafes, and fancy restaurants, she was dimly aware of the approving glances she was getting from the men she passed. At one time, just a smile from a cute guy would have sent her into a spasm of ecstasy. Even if she never learned the guy's name, she could have fantasized about him for days. It was so nice, now, to be firmly grounded in reality. She had Josh, and she didn't care about anyone else.

The Strand gave way to the business district, blocks of small offices and coffee shops. Near the center of a block of brick buildings was one indistinguishable from the rest except for a small, hand-lettered sign above two large, grimy, picture windows. Crisis Hotline—Help When You Need It, the sign said in uneven letters that had once been black but had since faded to a murky brown.

They definitely needed a new sign. Winnie thought that maybe that was why the hotline had so few volunteers. No one could find the place. She made a mental note to add a sign to the list of things they were going to buy with the money they raised from the benefit.

As Winnie pushed open the door, she heard the din of ringing telephones. *Brrring! Brrring!* All day and all night, the phones never stopped ringing, even though the hotline was only open ten hours a day. That was another thing they were hoping to do with the money they raised—pay the janitor, the only salaried employee of the hotline, to come in earlier and leave later so they could extend their hours.

"Winnie!" Teresa Gray called from the far end of the room where she sat at a long table behind a bank of phones. A graduate student in psychology at U. of S., Teresa ran the hotline with another grad student, David Arthur. David, thin and blond, sat further down the table, separated from Teresa by several empty chairs.

Barely breaking her pace, Winnie jogged across the dingy gray linoleum, past the hospital-green walls, to the battered, beige, Formica table. "Hi!" she greeted them, a little breathless from her run. "Where is everybody?"

"We're shorthanded as usual," Teresa said, pushing her wire-framed glasses up higher on her nose. Her dark brown hair was twisted up with a barrette, though loose tendrils escaped around her neck. Balanced on her shoulder was a beige receiver, connected by a spiral cord to a phone with a band of blinking red lights. Some flashed slowly and evenly, calls waiting to be answered, and some flashed rapidly, callers on hold.

"Let me pick up," Winnie said, bounding around the table to take an empty chair between Teresa and David.

"Actually," Teresa said, "we need to have a quick powwow about the benefit next week. Let me get off this call, then we'll just let the phones ring for a little while. Hopefully whoever's calling will keep trying."

After Teresa and David had hung up, David scooted down the table, closer to Winnie. His wispy blond hair was thinning in front, and his face was pale and doughy. He wore a brand new white T-shirt with a picture of a bright red phone off the hook, and the logo "The Hotline's Hot."

"Okay," David said tiredly, his voice hoarse from hours spent on the phone. He pulled a crumpled piece of paper from out of the back pocket of his pants and smoothed it on the table. "I made a list of all our fundraising ideas for the benefit. We're planning to sell T-shirts like the one I'm wearing, and refreshments, which we'll get some of our volunteers to provide at their own expense. But the main money's got to come from selling admission to the show—and the bigger the entertainment, the more we can charge."

"Any ideas who we can get to perform for us?" Teresa asked. "The best thing would be if we could get some big name singer or band to perform free in exchange for the publicity. Unfortunately, I don't know any famous people."

"Neither do I," Winnie said.

"Maybe we could get one of the local bands that play in the clubs around here," David suggested.

"I don't know what kind of a crowd that will pull," Teresa said, worriedly. "I wish I had more time to think about it, but between working here and my master's thesis . . ."

"Say no more," Winnie interrupted. *"I'll* take care of it. I have the time, and I'm not afraid to make a fool of myself, even if it means climbing in the window of some rock star's mansion and refusing to leave until he agrees to play for us. Of course, the rock star has to be within walking distance of the university, since I don't have a car, but trust me —I'll think of something."

Teresa laughed. "I'm sure you will. Thanks a lot. That really takes a load off my mind. We'll talk again after we close tonight. Back to work."

The phones hadn't stopped ringing the whole time they were talking. Winnie pressed the first flashing button and picked up the phone. "Crisis Hotline," she said in a friendly, professional voice. "What seems to be the problem?"

"Well, it's not a problem exactly," the girl said. "I'm just really tired all the time because so much is going on in my life right now. I'm waiting to hear which colleges have accepted me, I'm choreographing *and* directing the school play, I've got the lead in my ballet recital, plus I'm on the prom committee and the yearbook staff. Oh, and I have a weekend job at a shoestore at the mall."

"Wow," Winnie said. "Sounds like you've taken on a lot."

"Oh, I can handle it," the girl insisted in a shaky voice. "I've always been good at everything I've tried. My parents are always bragging to their friends about me. Did I mention I also get really good grades and that I run marathons in my spare time?" The girl's voice, which had been getting shakier, suddenly cracked and she burst into tears.

"Okay, okay," Winnie soothed her. "Go ahead and cry. You must be totally exhausted."

"My life is out of control," the girl sobbed. "I can hardly sleep at night, and I'm having trouble breathing. One minute I'm laughing hysterically, the next minute I'm crying my eyes out. I think I'm going crazy or something."

"You're not going crazy," Winnie said. "But it does sound like you've always tried to please your parents by being a super-achiever. Is that right?"

"I like to make them proud of me," the girl said.

"That's good," Winnie said. "But maybe you've gone a little overboard. You don't have to be the best at everything for your parents to love you. And you certainly don't want to run yourself into the ground. Then you won't be able to do *anything*."

"I'm certainly not functioning too well right now," the girl admitted. "I just feel like hiding in bed under the covers. I don't even want to go to school."

Winnie thought back to a few short months ago, when her own life seemed to be bursting at the seams. While she'd never been an over-achiever, she, too, had driven herself into a frenzied state, bouncing between two boyfriends, cutting classes, going on wild junk food binges, and mostly feeling totally lost and directionless.

Things had started to change when she'd wandered into the Crisis Hotline. She now knew that she wanted to major in psychology and become a therapist like her mother. Finding a focus had calmed her down a lot and had made it easier to deal with the rest of her life. Now all her relationships were going well —with Josh, her roommate Melissa, and with her two best friends from high school, Faith Crowley and KC Angeletti—and Winnie was determined that her life would never fall apart again.

"Here's what I think," Winnie said. "I think you need to pare down some of your activities. Maybe drop out of some of those committees or work fewer hours at your job. You don't have to do something every minute. Give yourself a little free time to just *be*."

The girl drew in a shaky breath. "I don't really need the money from my job," she said. "My parents give me a nice allowance. And I guess I don't have to work on the yearbook or the prom."

"Sounds better already," Winnie said encouragingly.

"But what will my parents say?" the girl demanded. "They'll think I'm goofing off."

"I think they'll be happier to have a daughter who's productive and cheerful than one who's having a nervous breakdown," Winnie said. "Talk to them about it. I bet they'll be very understanding when you explain how you feel."

The girl sighed. "I hope so. Can I call you back if it's still a problem?"

"Of course," Winnie said.

"What's your name?" the girl asked.

"I can't give you my whole name," Winnie said, "but my initials are W.G. Just ask for me next time you call."

"Thanks, W.G.," the girl said. "I already feel a lot better."

Winnie hung up and was about to answer another call when Teresa motioned to her to wait. "You have a personal call waiting," she said. "Line three."

"I do?" Winnie asked, surprised. Her close friends and mother knew she worked at the hotline, but they also knew not to call unless it was an emergency. "I hope nobody's had an accident," Winnie said, pressing the red flashing button. "Crisis Hotline," Winnie said automatically.

There was silence on the other end of the line. Was someone playing a joke on her? Or maybe the caller, tired of waiting, had hung up.

"Is anybody there?" Winnie asked.

"Uh . . . yes, I'm here," said a man's hesitant voice. He didn't sound young, but he didn't sound old, either. He only sounded nervous. "Winnie, is that you?"

"Yes," Winnie said, confused. How did he know her first name? Winnie never gave it out to anyone. That meant this man must know her, but his voice didn't sound familiar.

The man took a deep breath. "Okay," he said, "I'm sure you're going to think it's really strange hearing from me after all this time, but when I heard you were a student at the University of Springfield, I called your room, and your roommate told me you were working here. She warned me not to disturb you, but I thought after all these years I couldn't wait another minute to get in touch with you."

The more the man said, the more Winnie began to get a weird, tight feeling in her stomach.

"Don't hate me," the man went on. "Well, how could you hate me since the last time you saw me, you were only two years old? You probably don't even remember me, do you? I remember you, though. You were such a cuddly baby with little tufts of black hair sticking up all over your head and a cute little toothless grin. You were always smiling and bouncing on my knee. It's been one of the biggest regrets of my life that I never got to watch you grow up and see what kind of person you turned out to be, but I hope it's not too late. I'd like to see you, Winnie. I'd like to know you again."

Winnie could hardly breathe. There was no question in her mind who this man was, but she wanted to hear him say it. She wanted to be sure. "Who are you?" Winnie whispered.

"Winnie," the man said, "this is your father."

Two

•••••••••••••••••••

"ou can run, but you can't hide," sang the cheerful voice piped in over the radio loudspeakers at the U. of S. student union that afternoon.

"Story of my life," Faith Crowley said to KC Angeletti as the two pored over their Western Civilization textbooks at a rickety round table. Dozens of identical tables were spread over the broad space, divided every so often by concrete pillars, and lit by harsh, overhead fluorescent lights. At one end of the room was an aluminum snack bar that sold cellophane-wrapped tuna fish and baloney sandwiches and tiny, shiny bags of potato chips.

Faith bit hungrily into her tuna fish sandwich,

even though the bread was stale and the mayonnaise had a slightly sour taste. "I feel like a refugee," she said, washing down the food with a swig of orange-ade from a paper drink box. "As you know, I'm trying to avoid my roommate, so I eat on the run because I'm afraid I'll see her in the dining commons, and I try to get back to my room after Liza's asleep, but that ends up being really late because she's a night owl. I end up taking naps in the library."

KC shook her head sympathetically as she sipped her mineral water. Her long dark hair was swept off her face with a wide, pink headband, exposing her high cheekbones, smooth, pale skin, and cool, gray eyes. She wore a pink turtleneck sweater dress that perfectly matched the headband and showed off her slender figure.

"I don't blame you for trying to avoid Liza," KC said, "but don't you think you're overdoing it? The girl's not a monster."

"Try sharing a room with her," Faith said, "then get back to me. I'm telling you, Liza is driving me crazy. I think she's even doing it on purpose. It's bad enough I have to see her in the few hours of the day when I can't avoid my room, but she's following me around like a private eye. She transferred into my acting class and, as everyone knows, she just about forced me to give her a part in the Follies."

Faith had been one of several drama students directing a segment of the U. of S. Follies several weeks ago. Originally, Faith had awarded a song and dance number to her next-door neighbor, dance major Kimberly Dayton. Liza Ruff, who'd just replaced Lauren Turnbell-Smythe as Faith's roommate, had been furious that she hadn't been cast in the show. So furious in fact, that she hadn't let Faith alone for a minute.

"Come on," KC said reasonably. "You admitted yourself that you let Liza be Kimberly's understudy just to shut her up. And it all turned out great. Kimberly couldn't go on, and Liza was the hit of the show."

"Fine, fine, I'm not begrudging her her success," Faith said, anxiously twisting the end of her golden braid. "She saved me by coming through so well. But that doesn't mean I have to spend every minute of every day with her. I just wish she wouldn't hang around me so much."

"I guess she doesn't have any friends," KC said. "That's sort of sad."

"I used to feel sorry for her, too," Faith said. "And I've tried to be nice to her, but the minute I act even a little friendly, she jumps all over me and tries to take over my life. She wants to eat every meal with me and makes me describe every detail of every project I'm working on. It's exhausting. I've begged Lauren to hang out in our room, just so there'll be someone else there to distract Liza's attention from me. Lauren promised she would, especially since she's a little lonely living off campus."

"Lauren and Liza?" KC laughed. "Somehow I can't picture the two of them together. Lauren's so quiet and polite and Liza's so . . ."

"Overwhelming?" Faith suggested.

KC nodded. "Liza will swallow her up." She started to reach for one of Faith's potato chips, but her hand stopped in midair and quickly returned to her lap.

"Go ahead," Faith said. "Help yourself."

"No," KC said. "I shouldn't. Do you know how many calories are in each one of those chips?"

"Not too many," Faith said. "Besides, what are you worried about? You've got a great figure. A few potato chips won't kill you." Crumpling up the cellophane wrapper from the sandwich she'd just finished, Faith quickly unwrapped another one and bit off a huge chunk.

"They won't kill me," KC said, "but they might show up on camera next week when I'm modeling a Yuki Nikoto bikini."

"What?" Faith asked, taken aback for a minute. "Do you mean to tell me you've already gotten a modeling job? The agency signed you less than a week ago!" KC, who was always strapped for cash, had decided to model to help pay for new clothes and dues for her sorority, Tri Beta. She'd gone on interviews at two local agencies and one, Springfield Faces, had signed her immediately.

"I know," KC said, her gray eyes glittering with nervous energy. "I wasn't expecting anything to happen so soon, but they sent some of my pictures to the fashion editor at *Western* magazine, and the editor liked my look. And get this—the shoot's going to take place right on campus, at the indoor pool. Isn't that convenient?"

"That's great!" Faith said. "Wow, KC, you're such a multi-talented success. You're a future business leader of America, you're pledging the most prestigious sorority on campus, you're going out with a great guy, and now you're going to be a fashion model, on top of everything else. Can I have your autograph before you forget me?"

KC laughed and shook her head. "Don't envy me," she said. "I know it all sounds terrific, and it is, but meanwhile I'm a nervous wreck. There just aren't enough hours in the day for all the things I have to do. Between meetings and dinners at Tri Beta, homework and papers and special tutoring sessions to keep up my grades, and trying to find a little time to spend with Peter, I don't know when I'm going to be able to fit in this modeling thing."

"Oh, but you've got to," Faith said. "It sounds so glamorous!"

"It's not the glamour that I'm interested in," KC said. "It's the money. This job next week pays seventy bucks an hour, and it's a three-hour shoot. Can you imagine? More than two hundred dollars for three hours work? That's more than I made in a week when I was waitressing. I'll finally be able to buy some decent dresses for all the formal parties coming up. I'm sure Courtney must be getting tired of lending me her clothes all the time." Courtney Conner was president of Tri Beta and a good friend of KC's.

"That is a lot of money," Faith said, stuffing a handful of potato chips in her mouth.

"Exactly," KC said. "So I can't afford to blow this job by showing up with even an ounce of flab anywhere on my body. And if that means practicing a little self-denial, that's what I'll do."

"I understand completely," Faith said, devouring the rest of her second sandwich.

No wonder I never see Faith in the dining commons, thought Liza Ruff as she watched Faith eating. *She fills herself up on junk food all day. I really should have a talk with her about her diet.*

Unseen by Faith or KC, Liza sat on an empty pool table in the game room right across the hall from the student union. The dimly lit room, its walls lined with rows of video games, was a brightly blinking carnival of Ninja Turtles, Pacmen and women, race car drivers, and sword-toting, bare-chested medieval warriors.

Liza had been following Faith around for weeks, and everywhere Faith went, people seemed happy to see her. Of course, Faith had come to U. of S. with a distinct advantage—she'd brought her best friends from high school, KC and Winnie, with her.

Liza hadn't known anyone when she got to U. of S., plus she'd arrived in the middle of the semester after everyone had already formed friendships. It was awfully hard to break into any of the cliques, especially since she'd been forced to live in an all-female study dorm until a space opened up in Cole-ridge Hall. You couldn't make friends in an all-female study dorm. You weren't even allowed to talk out loud!

Liza had been hoping things would change when she moved in with Faith. Faith had seemed like a ready-made friend. They were sharing a room, they had the same interest in theater, and Faith was even directing the show Liza wanted to be in. Liza had done everything she could think of to make Faith like her—she'd tried to spend time with her, she'd tried to get to know Faith's friends, she'd even transferred into Faith's acting class so they'd have more to talk about. But no matter what she did, Faith seemed to shy away from her.

What would it take to get through to her? Liza wasn't going to give up. If anything, she was more determined than ever to break through Faith's shell. She just had to be aggressive. That's how she'd succeeded at everything else.

Back in New York, when she was just sixteen, Liza had decided she wanted to be a famous recording artist and movie star. Unfortunately, she didn't know anybody even remotely connected to show business since her father owned a shoe repair shop and her mother was secretary to an insurance broker.

Liza had decided that her best shot was to go to California, because she'd heard there were more opportunities there. But her parents had this silly idea that she should go to college, for the simple reason that they'd never gone. All their lives they'd saved up to send her, and she didn't have the heart to say no. She'd chosen U. of S. because it was supposed to have a good drama program, plus it was in the west. At least that was *near* California. After she graduated, she wouldn't have far to go.

It hadn't been a bad move, either. In just a few short months, she'd made a name for herself in the drama department and on campus. Everywhere she went, people recognized her because they'd either seen her in the Follies or on the TV news during *Week at the U.* Of course, no one stopped to chat for very long.

But it was all going to change soon. Liza was determined. All she had to do was keep pushing herself on Faith and Faith's friends, and she'd win them over. She'd make them see what a great person she was. And now was as good a time as any to wage another battle in her campaign.

Easing herself off the pool table, Liza plunked down on her stiletto-heeled pumps and swished across the hall with rapid steps. *I never should have worn these heels,* Liza thought. Her feet had swollen from half a day of trailing Faith all over campus, but Liza wasn't going to let that stop her. She'd walk barefoot, if that's what it took.

Faith and KC seemed deeply engrossed in their conversation. KC looked cool and elegant in her headband and matching dress. Faith was wearing her brown suede jacket with the fringe, a denim jumper, and cowboy boots. It wasn't a bad look if you worked at a rodeo, but if Faith wanted to be in show biz, she'd have to jazz herself up. That was another thing Liza would have to talk to her about.

Weaving between the round tables, Liza came to a halt in front of Faith and KC. "Hi!" she said brightly, steadying herself against the table, her long, red fingernails clicking against the enamel.

Faith had been smiling and laughing as she talked to KC, but the joy left her eyes as soon as she saw Liza. "Hi," she said in a tone of forced friendliness.

Liza felt a lump rise in her throat. Why did Faith dislike her so much? "Mind if I join you?" she asked.

Without waiting for an answer, Liza pulled up a chair, sat down, and tried to cross her legs, but her bright orange pedal pushers were too tight.

"So!" Liza said, folding her hands on the table and looking enthusiastically from Faith to KC. "What's new?"

"Not too much," Faith said, pressing her lips together and sneaking a quick look at KC.

Liza pretended she hadn't noticed. "There's got to be *something* new," she insisted. "How's your modeling career coming, KC? Faith told me you were signed by Springfield Faces."

KC nodded politely. "I just got my first job," she said.

Now here was something Liza could sink her teeth into. Modeling was just a step away from acting. After all, a camera was a camera. What difference did it make if you were moving or standing still? Maybe KC would be able to relate to her now.

"That's very exciting," Liza said. "What kind of a job is it?"

"I'm going to be modeling bathing suits for *Western* magazine," KC said. "They're doing an editorial spread on the designer Yuki Nikoto."

"Wow!" Liza said. "I've heard of her. She's married to Nick Nife of that rock group, Sound and Fury. Do you think Nick will be at the shoot?"

"I really don't know," KC said. "I don't even know if Yuki will be there."

"Where's it going to be?" Liza asked. "And when? I'd love to stop by."

"Uh . . . I don't think it's open to the public," KC said. "In fact, I really have to be going now. I've got to help cut out paper flowers for the Tri Beta tea. Courtney's expecting me." KC hurriedly pushed back her metal chair, gathered her books, and rose, tall and regal, above them. "See you later."

Faith looked after KC longingly like she, too, wanted to make a quick exit. Then she turned to Liza with a guilty look. "She really did have to go," Faith explained.

"Oh, I understand *completely,*" Liza said with a fluttering motion of her hand. "But that's perfectly all right because it will give the two of us more time to chat!"

Faith smiled weakly. Liza knew Faith wanted to

talk to her about as much as she wanted to drop out of school. But Liza wasn't fazed. She wasn't a quitter, and she certainly wasn't a shrinking violet.

"So listen, Faith," Liza said, "I've got this great idea for a two-woman show, and I thought it would be a perfect project for you and me."

Three

••••••••••••••••••••

"**T**his is amazing!" said a muscular young man with dark, curly hair. "This is absolutely incredible! I can't believe I'm seeing this!"

"They're hot!" his blond girlfriend agreed. "This is definitely going to go down in the history books."

Lauren Turnbell-Smythe, sitting behind the couple in the U. of S. gym, could barely hear them over the cheering crowd. On the shiny wooden floor in front of them, poised like jack-in-the-boxes about to spring, the U. of S. men's volleyball team watched as their server bashed the ball over the net like a deadly missile. On the other side of the net, the athletes from Medford College stood by helplessly as the scuffed, gray ball hit the floor at thirty miles an hour.

"Ten-zero!" the curly-haired young man crowed as the home crowd went wild. "If they keep it up, this will be their tenth shut-out in a row!"

"And their fifteenth straight victory," his girlfriend reminded him.

Lauren, her notebook open in front of her, jotted down these statistics among her other notes describing the purple-and-gold-uniformed giants that made up the U. of S. team.

Lauren had never been very interested in sports, and no one at the *Weekly Journal* expected her to cover this event, but Lauren had given herself the assignment. She saw it as a challenge, as a way of improving her skills as a reporter—and also as a way to keep busy. Her boyfriend, Dash Ramirez, hadn't been feeling well the past few days, so they hadn't spent much time together. Plus, living alone off-campus made it difficult for Lauren to see her friends. Covering the volleyball game seemed like a good way to do something constructive and be with people at the same time. It was hard to shake off the blues, though, and get caught up in the excitement of the team's winning streak.

Lauren's eyes wandered over the sea of animated faces, the waving triangles of purple and gold, the slow shuffling movement of people milling around the entrances to the gym. Lots of people had popped in to watch the game from the sidelines. Directly beneath Lauren, clustered by the door to the outdoor stadium, was a group of young women in purple and gold warm-up suits. Lauren recognized one of them by her bright red hair—it was Winnie's roommate, Melissa. Melissa watched the game with a serious expression, her arms crossed over her chest, reacting only slightly as U. of S. won another point.

"Hi!" Lauren said, dangling her fingers in front of Melissa's face.

Melissa looked up and smiled. "What are you doing here?" she shouted above the roaring crowd.

"I'm covering the game for the *Journal*," Lauren started to explain, but it was difficult to make herself heard over the noise. "Just a second," she said. "I'll come down."

Lauren slipped her knapsack over one shoulder and tucked her notebook and pen into the pocket of her patched jeans. Then she trotted down the wooden stairs to Melissa.

"I'm covering the game for the *Journal*," Lauren repeated. "Or, at least, I'm trying to. I've never done a sports story before."

"I'm sure it's like anything else," Melissa said. "Just tell 'em who won and what the score was and who got into a fight with whom. Sports fans love that."

"What are you doing here?" Lauren asked. "Are you a volleyball fan?"

"Not usually," Melissa said, "but I heard about this incredible winning streak, and I have a track meet in an hour, so I thought I'd stop by for a little while. I heard that if they win this game, they'll set a new school record for the most consecutive wins. That's got to be a lead story for your paper, right?"

"Right," Lauren said. "Let's just hope they win."

The Medford coach blew his whistle and called a time-out. The U. of S. crowd booed as he walked out onto the court to talk to his team.

"Guess he's trying to regroup," Melissa said.

"So how's Winnie doing?" Lauren asked. "Faith told me she heard from her father after all these years. She must be in shock."

"She *was* surprised," Melissa said, "but she seems to be taking it very calmly, which surprises me. I remember when she used to go crazy over the slightest little thing. And this is big, really big. But she's acting so blasé about it."

"That is surprising," Lauren agreed. "I guess Winnie's changed a lot recently. She seems much more mellow."

"Winnie sure seems to think so," Melissa said wryly.

"So what's she going to do about her father?" Lauren asked. "Is she going to see him?"

"She didn't want to at first," Melissa said, "but she finally agreed to meet him tomorrow."

Lauren shook her head, and her wispy, light brown hair floated softly around her face. "I can't believe she didn't want to see him. If I hadn't seen *my* father in over sixteen years, I'd be *dying* to meet him. There'd be so many questions I'd want to ask him, like why he left in the first place, and why he decided to look me up after all that time. Doesn't Winnie seem even a little bit curious? Doesn't she want to know what he looks like?"

"Nope." Melissa reached up to the bleachers above her head and hooked her fingers over the edge. Then she lifted her feet off the ground so that she was suspended, stretching out her upper body. "Ahhhh," she sighed. "That feels great."

"Come on," Lauren persisted. "She's got to seem nervous or excited or something."

Melissa shook her head. "Winnie says he's not a part of her life. She already knows what he's like from her mother—a good-for-nothing, untrustworthy lout."

The sound that welled up in the gym was unlike anything Lauren had ever heard. It didn't sound like a thousand human voices united in euphoria.

And no wonder, the U. of S. men's volleyball team had just won their fifteenth straight victory.

"We missed it," Lauren yelled over the noise. "I should have been watching the last few minutes of the game." Above her head, hundreds of feet stomped on the wooden bleachers in glee.

"Just talk to the players," Melissa suggested. "I'm sure they'll be happy to give you a play-by-play."

"You're right," Lauren said, whipping out her notebook and uncapping her pen.

Fans were pouring down the bleachers and filling the court, jumping on top of the U. of S. players, pounding them on the back, and lifting them in the air.

"This is ridiculous!" Lauren declared. "Here it is, the sports story of the semester, and I won't be able to get anywhere near them."

"I know where you can find them," Melissa said. "Follow me." She broke a path through the mass of bodies, and wound her way across the court, and under the net.

Lauren had a hard time keeping her in view, and was distressed to see the purple-and-gold uniformed players disappear through a big steel door in the side wall of the gym.

"Here we are," Melissa said when the two girls had also reached the door.

"Where are we?" Lauren asked as several more

sweaty, muscular young men in purple shorts brushed past them and went through the door.

"It's the men's locker room. Just go inside, and you'll get all the interviews you need."

Lauren's violet eyes widened behind her wire-rimmed glasses. "What?" she asked, her voice soft and breathy.

"I said, just go into the locker room and talk to the players."

Lauren froze. "I can't do that," she whispered. "That's a locker room! That means guys are getting undressed in there! It would be indecent of me to talk to them while they're . . . well, you know."

Melissa shrugged. "Suit yourself. But I don't know any other way you'll be able to get them all in one place at one time. You'll have to go running all over campus to look for them, and you won't get the flavor of the post-game excitement. Reporters like to put that in their articles, right?"

"Right, but going in the locker room can't be the only way to interview athletes."

"Actually, it isn't," Melissa said, pondering. "After our track meets, we meet the reporters at a public reception area."

"Oh!" Lauren said, relieved. "Then that's where I'll go."

Melissa shook her head. "I was talking about the *women's* track team. The men's track team doesn't have a reception area. I don't think any of the men's teams do."

"Excuse me! Excuse me!" a pudgy young man shouted loudly, as he made his way through the crowd. Lauren recognized him as Charlie Mandelkern, a regular sports reporter for the *Weekly Journal.* He was chewing gum loudly and clutched a tiny microcassette recorder in his chubby hand. "Excuse me! Excuse me! Press!" he announced importantly, pushing right past Lauren and Melissa and barging into the men's locker room.

The steel door slammed in Lauren's face with a boom that reverberated through her bones. Lauren stared at the cold, gray surface of the door and felt a chill creep up her spine. Obnoxious Charlie Mandelkern, who could barely spell, let alone put a decent sentence together, was going to get the inside scoop on the volleyball story while she was left out in the cold. Lauren was determined to find out why the men's teams didn't have a reception area for reporters. And she was determined to be more brazen next time—that is if she bothered to come to the next volleyball game at all.

Four

....

Melissa's chest broke through the white tape at the finish line, and the crowd roared its approval. Feeling loose, light, and out of breath, she continued to jog around the eight-lane oval of the U. of S. stadium. While Melissa didn't think she'd broken any records for the 800 meters, she knew she'd run a good race, a smart race. She'd stayed with the pack for the first lap around the track, then poured on the speed at the end, overtaking first the top runner from Roseburg University, then her nemesis and teammate, Caitlin Bruneau.

Caitlin, a junior, had tried to psych Melissa out earlier in the year. She'd almost convinced Melissa that she couldn't be a track star *and* have a relationship with a guy at the same time. Melissa wanted to kick herself now for believing Caitlin. The past few months with Brooks had been the most wonderful in her life. He'd been the first guy she'd ever trusted, the first person she'd ever truly opened up to, and he'd come through for her every time. He was warm and caring and totally dependable; he was everything her alcoholic, unemployed father wasn't. Being with Brooks had healed a lot of Melissa's wounds.

"Melissa!" Brooks's voice rose above the fading cheers as Melissa finished her victory lap. She saw him running toward her from the stands, his blond curls glistening in the late afternoon sunlight. His rugged, handsome face was lit up with joy, and his sturdy arms were open wide. Melissa ran right into his arms, and nestled her face against the soft flannel of his shirt.

"My champion," he murmured, holding her close. "You were beautiful out there. Like a force of nature. Nobody else even came close."

Melissa felt incredibly lucky. Everything in her life was going so well now. She had Brooks, she'd been winning consistently in track, and her grade point average was a solid 3.8—more than enough to get into a good medical school.

Caitlin Bruneau, eat your heart out! Melissa

thought as she and Brooks passed the frizzy-haired junior, arm in arm. Caitlin stood with their track coach, Terry Meeham. The two were talking so quietly Melissa couldn't hear what they were saying, but Caitlin had a tense look on her face.

"Legs!" Terry called out to Melissa as they passed, his lean face lighting up in a smile. "You want to take a guess?" he asked, holding up one of the three electronic stopwatches that always hung around his neck.

"I know I didn't break one-fifty," Melissa said. "One minute fifty-one seconds?"

Terry grinned. "One-fifty-point-five-two," he said. "Very close to your personal best. Keep it up, McDormand."

Melissa smiled and hugged Brooks around his solid waist. "Thanks, coach. See you at practice tomorrow."

Melissa retrieved her nylon warm-up suit from the side of the track and pulled it on. Then, taking hold of Brooks's hand, she led him across the lawn surrounding the gymnasium/stadium complex. The grass, fresh and green, felt spongy beneath her sneakers. The distant, snow-topped mountains zigzagged against the cloudless, blue sky.

"So," Brooks said, letting his lips brush softly against her cheek. "What shall we do to celebrate your victory?"

Melissa felt a wave of pleasure flow through her body at the touch of his lips. "Hmmm . . ." she said, pretending to think. "That's a very good question."

"Maybe we'd better discuss it *privately,* " Brooks said, running his hands lightly down the curve in her lower back.

"I think that would be best," Melissa said as grass gave way to the cobbled bricks of McLaren Plaza. Cherry trees in full bloom dotted the square, filling the air with their sweet, light fragrance. In the center, stood a cast-iron statue of Derwood C. Brock, the founding president of U. of S.

Brooks paused to pick up a pale pink cherry blossom that had fallen on the bricks, then he ran its silky petals down Melissa's nose. "Where would you like to go?" he asked, his voice husky.

All Melissa wanted was to pull Brooks to her again, to feel his body close to hers, to run her hands through his curls and cover his face with kisses. But Brooks was right. They couldn't start mauling each other in the middle of McLaren Plaza.

"I wish we could go to my room," Melissa said, "but we'll just get interrupted when Winnie comes home. And I don't want to make her mad again by hogging the room."

"Yeah," Brooks agreed. "We promised we'd try to

be more considerate. Anyway, it's kind of messy in there with all her candy wrappers and dirty clothes and papers all over the floor. Doesn't that drive you crazy sometimes? You're so neat and she's such a packrat."

"I don't love it," Melissa said, "but I'm getting used to it. I'm more worried that Winnie will come in and start motor-mouthing about some new flavor of Doritos, which will remind her of this funny story from when she and KC and Faith had a slumber party in junior high school, and on, and on, and on. Not exactly mood music for a romantic evening."

"Okay," Brooks said, resting his muscular forearms on Melissa's shoulders and tickling the back of her neck with his fingers. "How about my room?"

"Barney's bound to be there," Melissa said, referring to Brooks's roommate. "He studies there, he works out there, he even eats there sometimes. If he didn't have to go somewhere else for classes, he'd never leave!"

"That's true," Brooks admitted. "He's a great guy, but I'm always tripping over his weight bench and barbells. I don't know why he can't use the gym like everyone else."

"Which still leaves us with no place to go," Melissa sighed, turning her head to kiss Brooks's fingertips.

"Not necessarily," Brooks said.

"What do you mean?"

"Walk with me," Brooks said, slipping his hand across her shoulders and heading toward the sculpture garden adjoining the plaza. The garden, surrounded by a wrought iron fence, was a gently sloping lawn with marble statues of graceful, lifelike animals, humans, and fantastical creatures. A curving gravel path, lined with cement benches, connected the odd menagerie. Brooks opened the gate and they stepped onto the winding path.

"I've been thinking," Brooks began as their feet clicked against the smooth, white stones beneath them, "I've been through a lot this year. I've been plunged into the toughest academic situation of my life. When I was in high school, good grades came easily to me. Then I started at the Honors College here, and I suddenly felt—well—scared that I couldn't cut it. That I wasn't smart enough. That I couldn't even *pass*, let alone do well. But I've proved myself. I've adapted, and now my grades are strong."

Brooks stopped to admire a statue of a stallion. It stood on its hind legs, its forelegs kicking the air, its mane waving in an unseen wind. Melissa couldn't tell what Brooks was getting at, or what this had to do with their lack-of-privacy problem, but she waited patiently, knowing he'd get to the point before long.

"I've been through a lot emotionally, too," Brooks went on. "When Faith and I broke up at the beginning of the semester, I thought I was going to fall apart. We'd dated for four solid years, all through high school, and suddenly she dumps me when we get to college. So here I was, in this totally new place, without anyone to depend on. But I got through it. I got over her—completely. Then I met you."

Melissa still didn't see the connection, but she could sense Brooks was getting to the point. She allowed him to lead her to a cement bench, and they sat down on the hard surface, still warm from the afternoon sun.

"You and I have had our ups and downs, too," Brooks continued. "You had such a hard shell, at the beginning. I wasn't sure if I'd ever get through to you. But I did, and I felt something I never felt with Faith, or anyone else. Even that time you told me you never wanted to see me again, I never stopped loving you. And ever since we got back together, I've been so sure about us. I can feel it in every cell of my body. We belong together."

Brooks took Melissa's hands in his own and she felt the gentle pressure of his strong fingers. She closed her eyes and sighed happily.

"My whole point," Brooks said, "is that after everything I've been through, I've realized something important about myself. I'm really ready, now, to make a commitment to someone—to you."

Melissa opened her eyes. Was Brooks saying he wanted them to see each other exclusively? She thought they already were. She wasn't seeing anybody else. Was he trying to say he'd been dating other girls while he'd been seeing her? "I thought we already had a commitment," she said warily.

"Of course we have," Brooks said, allaying her fears, "but I'm talking about something more than that. I've figured out a way for us to be together *all* the time, without having to worry about roommates or interruptions."

Melissa looked up at Brooks in confusion. "What do you mean?"

Brooks squeezed her hand and looked at her unblinkingly. "How would you feel about sharing an apartment?" he asked.

"With you?" Melissa asked, not believing what she was hearing.

"Of course with me," Brooks answered.

Melissa's mind expanded and contracted, flipped and flopped as she tried to make sense of Brooks's words. *Share an apartment? Live together?* Melissa loved Brooks. She was just as sure of her feelings for him as he was for her, but never in a million years would she have considered taking such a huge step at this point in her life. They were only college freshmen! Before this year, Melissa had never lived away from home, let alone moved in with a boyfriend. In fact, she'd never even *had* a boyfriend, before Brooks. Was she old enough, or mature enough, to seriously consider Brooks's suggestion?

"Well?" Brooks asked, his expression serene. He didn't seem to share any of Melissa's doubts.

Melissa didn't know what to say. She needed time to think. "Well," she said, "there are a number of factors to be considered. For one thing, I'm on a track scholarship, which requires that I live on campus. I don't really know how we could get around that since we'd have to find an apartment in town."

Brooks smiled. "I'm sorry. I guess I didn't make myself clear. I didn't mean that we should find an apartment off campus and move in together. I was talking about *married* students' housing."

Now Melissa was really confused. How could she and Brooks move into married students housing unless they were . . .

Melissa searched Brooks's face for some sign that he was joking. Or maybe he'd meant something else and she'd misunderstood him. But Brooks continued to look at her calmly.

"You're not asking me to ma-a—" Melissa was too

embarrassed to even say the word, for fear he'd laugh when he heard it.

"Of course I am," Brooks said. "So? What do you say?"

If Melissa hadn't been sitting on the bench, she might have fallen face down in the gravel. She began to feel dizzy, and statues of horses, dogs, nymphs, and centaurs began to spin around her head. The scent of nearby cherry blossoms nearly choked her with their sweetness.

There could be no more question about it— Brooks had just proposed!

Five

"**U**ntil the sixteenth century, most of Europe was united in the same religious faith. Though heresies cropped up from time to time during the Middle Ages, most Christians continued to recognize the authority of the papacy in Rome." Professor Hermann, Winnie's Western Civilization professor, droned on, pausing occasionally to push his bifocals further up on his bulbous nose. His monotone voice reminded Winnie of a hypnotist. "The only exceptions were the Greek and Russian Orthodox . . ."

Winnie felt her eyelids droop, but she forced herself to sit upright and hold her pen tighter as she continued taking notes. It didn't help that the lecture hall was sweltering hot, with sunlight pouring through the windows. It didn't help that, to her right, KC was surreptitiously polishing her nails a subtle shade of peach. It didn't help that Faith, on her left, was quietly munching on Cheddar Cheese Bugles and getting orange powder all over her pen and notebook. And it didn't help that to Faith's left, Lauren was hunched over a typewritten manuscript, occasionally scribbling on it or crossing something out with a red pen. It was probably something she'd written for her Creative Writing class.

Most of all, it didn't help that Winnie had barely slept a wink for the past two nights. She hadn't been able to stop thinking and worrying about what was going to happen at three o'clock this afternoon. Winnie was mad at herself for her lack of self-control. She was going to see her father today. It was no big deal. It wasn't like he'd played an important role in her life or anything. In fact, he hadn't played *any* role. He was a perfect stranger. So why was she letting herself get agitated over meeting him?

"However, the overall unity was rudely shattered by the movement that has come to be known as the Protestant Reformation," Professor Hermann continued, lifting a page of his lecture notes and flipping it over.

Winnie tried to screen out everything except her

professor's voice, but strange images kept appearing in her mind. Laughing, dark eyes, a hollow plastic rattle shaped like a pink elephant with purple polka dots, and a squeaky voice singing "We all live in a yellow submarine" all swirled before her. These couldn't be memories. She'd been far too young when her father went away to remember anything about him. She was probably hallucinating because she was overtired.

Winnie fought back the images. She didn't want to let some phantom of a father disrupt her peace of mind—not when everything was finally exactly how she wanted it.

Professor Hermann cleared his throat, forcing Winnie back to attention. "That concludes today's lecture," he said. "For next time, please read the chapter on the Protestant Reformation."

Winnie got up. She checked her watch. It was two-thirty. She had more than enough time to get to the boat house by Mill Pond where she'd told her father she'd meet him. But she wanted to run there as fast as she could. The sooner she saw him, the sooner she could get it over with. Winnie climbed the stairs of the lecture hall two at a time.

"Hey!" Faith called after her. "Why the rush?"

Winnie shrugged as she paused. "I've got an appointment," she said. "It's nothing major, I just don't want to be late."

"With your Russian history professor?" Faith asked. "Are you going to argue for a better grade on that paper you just got back? Not that an A-minus is anything to sneeze at."

"Yeah," KC laughed, catching up to them. "If *I'd* gotten an A-minus, I'd kiss the professor's feet, but if you thought you deserved an A, then I'm sure you did."

"Actually," Winnie hedged, "I'm not meeting my professor."

Lauren, trudging up the stairs behind Faith and KC gave Winnie a curious look. "Did you decide to meet your father?" she asked.

The alarmed look on Winnie's face was answer enough.

"Your *father?*" Faith shrieked, clutching Winnie's arm. "You're meeting your father and you say it's 'nothing major'? Why didn't you tell me you were seeing him today?"

"Yeah!" KC said indignantly. "You told us you'd spoken to him, but you never said anything about getting together."

"It's no big deal," Winnie insisted, once again climbing the stairs with her friends trailing behind her. "I didn't want to tell that many people."

"We're not people!" Faith cried. "We're your oldest living friends. I can't believe you didn't say anything."

"Me neither," KC said, hurt.

The girls passed through an old, wooden door into a dimly lit hallway and down the main staircase. Winnie waited until they were outside, on the grassy lawn, before she tried to explain.

"Don't be upset," she said to her friends. "I didn't mean to shut you out. It's just that this is something that's going to be over and done with in half an hour. I'm going to see him, say hello, say goodbye, and that's it."

"But he's your *father,*" Faith said. "How can you be so cut and dry about it?"

"He's my father in name only," Winnie said coldly. "He was never there for me when I needed him. I don't even *know* him. He can't expect me to just open up to him and love him sixteen years after he walked out on my mom and me."

KC gingerly patted Winnie's arm, keeping her still-wet fingernails bent upward. "I guess I see your point," she said. "But try not to be too hard on him. At least listen to what he has to say."

"Oh, I'll listen," Winnie assured them. "I won't be interested, but I'll listen."

"Will you at least call us afterward and tell us what happened?" Lauren asked.

"Sure," Winnie said. "But there won't be much to say." She looked at her watch again. "It's a quarter to three. I'd better be going." She took off at a trot, her carpetbag full of books banging against her psychedelic leggings as she ran.

"Call us!" Faith reminded her again as Winnie climbed up the grassy hill to the dirt bike path that led to Mill Pond.

Though the sun was shining brightly overhead, the bike path was dark and slightly damp under the constant shade of the leafy trees around it. Long ruts left by bicycle tires crisscrossed the densely packed earth. Overgrown grass crept over the edge of the path, and an occasional squirrel or chipmunk scurried past when it thought no one was looking.

Keeping to the side of the path and dodging the occasional biker, Winnie started to jog toward Mill Pond. The closer she got, the heavier her feet felt. Her whole body felt like it was turning to lead. Winnie slowed down as the pond came into view.

Mill Pond was irregularly shaped, and surrounded by willow trees, which trailed their graceful branches into the water like strands of pale green hair. The water rippled as a mother duck swam past, obediently followed by a line of paddling ducklings. Students cut noiselessly through the water in canoes.

Winnie hadn't chosen Mill Pond as a meeting place because it was beautiful or because it was a quiet place to talk. Winnie had chosen it because she knew there would be people around and because it was out in the open. There was nothing intimate or personal about it. It was a public place where anybody could come. That should send the right message to her father. As far as Winnie was concerned, he was just anybody.

The boathouse was halfway around the pond. Next to it, canoes and rowboats were stacked in the sand that had been trucked in to create a small artificial beach. As usual, there was a line of people waiting to rent rowboats. A wide walkway lined with wooden benches led from the bike path down to the beach and the boathouse. The benches, too, were filled with people.

Winnie scanned the benches quickly for anyone who looked like he might be her father. She saw loving couples, students bent over books, and sunbathers in shorts and T-shirts, but there was no sign of a middle-aged man. Come to think of it, Winnie didn't know exactly how old her father was or even what he looked like. Her mother had destroyed all the pictures she had of him.

Remembering now the little her mother had told her about him, Winnie could understand why. Her parents had married young, right out of college. Winnie's mother had never been too specific about what Winnie's father had done for a living, except to say that he'd been some sort of a salesman and that he'd traveled a lot. The only other thing Winnie knew about him was that the divorce had been messy and he'd disappeared completely after that. He'd never tried to call her or visit her, and her mother had told her he'd never contributed any money for child support.

So where did this guy come off now, sixteen years later, trying to get to know her? The more Winnie thought about it, the angrier she felt. What did he want from her, anyway? Maybe he'd turned into some sort of bum and just wanted her to give him money. Well, Winnie knew what she'd say to that. *Get lost, creep! I don't owe you anything.*

Winnie sat down on an empty bench and impatiently tapped her muddy running sneakers on the pavement. Where was he already? It was exactly three o'clock. If he didn't show up in five minutes, Winnie decided, she was going to leave.

Looking up toward the bicycle path, Winnie spotted a young-looking man with longish, dark hair emerge from behind the trees. She glanced at him briefly, then turned her gaze to the professionally clad bikers with sleek, plastic helmets and shiny lycra shorts who zipped past him.

"Winnie?" asked a nervous, male voice.

Winnie looked up. The young-looking man with the dark hair stood directly in front of her, shading his eyes from the sun with his hand. He was slim, not too tall, with faded jeans, black lizard cowboy boots, a denim shirt, and a wide, cotton tie with swirling, psychedelic colors. His hairline was receding slightly, and he had a few crinkly lines at the corners of his eyes, but he didn't look more than forty years old. His eyes, even in the shade of his hand, twinkled, and his nearly manic smile reminded Winnie of someone she knew very well—someone she saw in the mirror every day.

"I'm Winnie," Winnie said coolly, proud of the fact that she really *felt* cool. Her heart wasn't beating any faster and she didn't feel nervous or excited or anything.

The man's grin grew even wider and he leaned forward to kiss her on the cheek. "Winnie!" he exclaimed happily. "It's me, dad!"

Winnie allowed him to kiss her, but she was stiff and unresponsive.

"Okay," the man said nervously, perching on the bench beside her. "I don't blame you for hating me. I'm sure I would feel the same way if I were in your position. You're probably thinking, *Hey, who does this guy think he is, popping up now after sixteen years? What kind of creep would leave his daughter and never try to call her or write her or even send her a birthday card?*"

"You must be a mindreader," Winnie said dryly. "But don't worry. I don't hate you. Hate implies some sort of strong emotion. I don't feel anything for you."

"Which is a whole lot worse," the man said, bouncing nervously on the bench. He jumped up and began to pace back and forth in front of Winnie. "But don't worry, you haven't hurt my feelings. My feelings don't matter much at this point, anyway. Go ahead, say anything you want to me. Get it out of your system. You want me to start you off? Okay, let's see, *Listen you jerk, I've got a lot better things to do than sit here and listen to you babble! You're scum, dad! You're slime! You're the lowest form of life on this planet, maybe lower."*

Winnie had the unsettling feeling that she was not only looking into a mirror—she was also listening to a tape recording of her voice! This guy—she still couldn't think of him as her father—walked like her, talked like her, dressed like her, and she didn't even know his name!

The man slapped himself on the side of his head with his hand. "I'm a bigger jerk than I thought," he said. "I didn't introduce myself. Of course you're not going to call me dad when you don't know me. I'm not sure if your mother even told you anything. My name is Byron Jennings." He held out his right hand for her to shake.

Winnie took it and shook it half-heartedly. "How do you do?" she said, with a grim half-smile.

"Better, now that I've seen you," Byron said, sitting down again on the other side of Winnie. "We look so much alike. Now I understand why people have children. It's to leave part of yourself behind after you've gone. But of course, that's just the cosmic connection between parents and children. There's a whole lot more to raising children which I've obviously missed. But I'd like to start making it up to you now, if you'll let me."

"Look," Winnie said, trying not to look into the dark eyes so much like her own. "You don't owe me anything. Or maybe you do, but I'm not the least bit interested in getting paid back now. It's too late. I don't owe *you* anything either. So if you're looking for some sort of comfort in your old age—not that you look old, but you know what I mean— you're looking in the wrong place."

"Why won't you give me a chance?" Byron asked. "You wouldn't even have to do anything, except let me explain where I've been all these years and why I never came looking for you."

"I'll tell you why," Winnie said, fighting to keep her voice level. "The only thing my mother ever said about you was that we were lucky to be rid of you. And since she's the one who was always there for me, she's the one I'm going to believe. Nothing you can do or say will make any difference to me."

"Please," Byron pleaded. "Don't walk away. Five

minutes more of your time is all I ask. Just let me talk."

Winnie crossed her arms in front of her chest. "Five minutes," she agreed. "After that, I have to go. I've got a very busy life."

"Which I'm dying to hear about," Byron said. "I mean, if you decide you want to tell me about it. But, okay, here I go. Your mother and I were very young when we got married. Too young. Neither one of us was really ready to settle down. But I take all of the blame. I was the impulsive one. I was the one who said we should jump in without thinking. And I guess I was too good a salesman, 'cause I talked your mother into it against her better judgment.

"We were happy, too, for a little while, but I had to travel a lot for my job, and your mother was very lonely. It was lonely for me too, though. I'll even admit there were a few times when I was on the road that I . . . well, never mind, that's really nothing you should hear about. Your mom became pregnant with you almost right away, and I thought that would make her happy. I thought you'd be enough to keep her company while I was away, but things just got worse and worse between us. We used to fight all the time. I guess you don't remember because you were so small.

"Do you remember *anything* about me? I know I

wasn't around much, but I used to bounce you on my knee and sing to you in funny voices to make you laugh. You were such a happy baby, you laughed at anything. You loved it when I sang one song in particular. 'We all live in a yellow submarine . . .' " he sang in a high-pitched falsetto.

Winnie felt her stomach flip over. Her chest felt tight, forcing her to take quick, shallow breaths. Winnie balled her hands into fists and dug her nails into her palms to take her mind off what she was hearing. She didn't need to hear this. She didn't want to hear this. And besides, his five minutes were up.

"Sorry," she said quickly, rising from the bench, "but I've really got to go."

Byron jumped up, too, and grabbed her arm. "Please," he said, "there's so much more I want to say."

"Look," Winnie said, prying his fingers off her arm, "I've done everything you asked. You wanted me to meet you, I met you. You wanted me to listen, I listened. As far as I'm concerned, there's nothing more you can say that will make me feel any different about you. So, nice to meet you, and goodbye."

Winnie started walking quickly up toward the bicycle path, already trying to put the memory of this man behind her.

"Winnie, wait! Please!" Byron implored her. "Don't say this is the end. At least say there's a chance we can talk again sometime."

Winnie ignored him and kept on walking.

"Okay," Byron said, "I understand why you're still angry. But don't close the door." He reached into his pocket for a business card and scribbled something on the back of it as he walked along beside her. "This is the name and phone number of my hotel in Springfield. I'll be here until a week from Monday. If you change your mind, call me anytime, day or night. I'll always be happy to hear from you."

Winnie didn't take the card, but she didn't stop him when he slipped it into her carpetbag.

"Goodbye, Winnie!" Byron called after her.

Winnie turned onto the hard-packed earth of the bike path and broke into a run. She wanted to get away from this man as fast as she could. Nothing he said made any difference to her. No matter how much he looked like her, acted like her, or thought like her, he was still a perfect stranger.

Six

"Ugh! I look like a scarecrow!" KC said to her boyfriend, Peter Dvorsky. "My hair looks like straw." She was staring at her reflection in the full-length mirror on the back of her closet door. Usually lustrous and thick, her dark hair was limp and dry. "It's all those split ends. Thank goodness I'm getting my hair cut today. Not that I really have time." KC opened her briefcase and pulled out her leather organizer. She flipped to the page for today, Saturday, which was filled with scribbled notes to herself. "I've got exactly one hour to get to the hairdresser, and on the way I've got to stop by the library to get a book on macroeconomic theory to help me with my econ test, then I've got to sign my contract at the agency because they close at one today, then I'm getting my haircut, then I've got to stop by Tri Beta for a meeting—we're making the decorations for Winnie's benefit for the Crisis Hotline—then I've got to write my essay, and I'd better do a good job because I don't have time to write any more extra credit papers—and *then*, if I have time, I'm going to collapse."

"You'll get it all done," Peter reassured her. "I know how organized you are."

He lay on KC's bed, his head propped up in his hand. His black jeans were so faded they were almost the same color as his stretched-out, gray U. of S. sweatshirt. His hair, a shade somewhere between light brown and blond, could also use a cut, KC noted, but she was too busy to worry about that right now.

"There's one thing I didn't hear you mention on your itinerary," Peter said, sitting up on KC's bed. "Lunch or dinner."

"I had a good breakfast this morning," KC said, searching for her English notebook in the neat pile on her desk. "Yogurt, a banana, and orange juice. That's more than enough."

"That's not enough to get you through such a busy day," Peter said, reaching under KC's bed for something.

"Who are you?" KC asked. "My mother?"

"I hope not," Peter said. His hand emerged from beneath the bed holding a small shopping bag.

"What's that?" KC asked as Peter reached into the bag and pulled out several oddly shaped objects wrapped in silver foil.

"Now, it's nothing elegant," Peter warned, pulling out a square of red-checked fabric from the bag and spreading it on KC's floor. Then he produced a thermos, a heavy china plate from the dining hall, and some silverware. "Sit down," he commanded her as he sat on the floor. He unwrapped the foil packages and arranged them on the plate. There was a peanut butter and jelly sandwich, some graham crackers, and an apple. The steaming Thermos held hot chocolate, which Peter poured into its red plastic cup.

KC's mouth began to water even before the rich, chocolatey aroma floated up toward her nostrils. The graham crackers were a crispy, golden brown, and the white dining commons bread looked soft and fresh. The apple gleamed in the sunlight coming in through the window.

It was so thoughtful of Peter to be concerned about her. She hadn't been eating much lately in her effort to slim down for her swimsuit spread. KC's modeling agent had told her some of the suits would be fairly revealing, and KC wanted her body to look perfect. There were sure to be other, far more experienced models at the shoot, and KC didn't want to seem like an amateur compared to them.

Then again, all this dieting had left her feeling tired and lightheaded. KC was tempted to taste a corner of the sandwich or a few bites of the apple. That shouldn't add up to too many calories. She started to reach for the shiny, red apple, then stood up abruptly.

"What's the matter?" Peter asked. "I know it's not caviar, but everything's fresh from the dining hall. I picked it up on my way here." Peter took half the sandwich off the plate and stood up in front of her. Since he was average height for a guy, and she was tall for a girl, they stood exactly eye to eye. Peter's hazel eyes were filled with love and concern.

"Nothing's wrong with the food," KC said, kissing him lightly on the tip of his nose. "I'm just not hungry right now."

"Don't give me that," Peter said, making his voice sound gruff. "You're starving to death before my very eyes, and I'm not going to stand here and let you do it. You're *my* girlfriend, and I'd like you strong and healthy, thank you very much."

KC's first impulse was to throw her arms around Peter and let him comfort and feed her. She could almost feel the warmth of his arms and the firmness of his chest and the gentle way he stroked her hair when he held her. She could taste the sticky sweetness of the peanut butter and feel the smooth warmth of the hot chocolate.

But KC held herself rigid and clamped her mouth shut. To give in to Peter would be showing weakness, dependence. She'd spent eighteen years doing things for herself without asking anyone, even her parents, for help. And she had a lot to show for it. She'd gotten into Tri Beta, the most exclusive sorority on campus, even though her mother and father were ex-hippies who owned a health food restaurant. She was embarking on a potentially lucrative modeling career, which could help pay for business school. She was also getting halfway decent grades through sheer willpower since she wasn't a naturally gifted student.

She couldn't let down her guard, just because she had a boyfriend. If she did, it would be too tempting to let herself go completely. If she let her emotions control her, she'd fall completely in love with Peter. She'd spend every free second with him, hugging, kissing, laughing, and eating. She'd be a happy, lazy blimp.

KC gave Peter a quick peck on the cheek, then backed away from him and the food. "Thanks," she said briskly, "but I assure you I am in no need of emergency assistance. I don't have time to eat, anyway. I've got to get to the library before someone else from my class swipes that macroeconomics book." KC tossed her English notebook and her economics textbook into her briefcase and snapped it shut.

Peter frowned as he knelt down by the plate and started wrapping up the food again. "Why don't you take something with you for later?" he suggested.

"Nope," KC said, striding to her closet and pulling on a navy blazer with gold buttons over her clean, white shirt and crisply pressed navy slacks.

Peter recapped the Thermos and threw everything back into the shopping bag. "At least let me give you a ride downtown," he said. "I've got my motorcycle parked right outside."

"You're a gem," KC said, picking up her briefcase, "but I've really got too many stops to make. I can't ask you to waste your whole afternoon chauffering me around."

"But really," Peter insisted, "I don't mi . . ."

"No thank you," KC said, hugging him quickly with her free arm. "Just shut the door behind you on your way out."

Peter turned off his motorcycle and parked it near the bike rack behind Rapids Hall, one of a series of plain, brick dorms which lined one side of the vast

U. of S. green. Peter's own dorm, Coleridge Hall, was also part of the complex.

Tucking his glossy, black motorcycle helmet under his arm, Peter pulled open the front door to Rapids Hall. He headed up the stairs for the common room where they were holding a meeting about the whitewater rafting trip scheduled for the following Saturday. Though he hardly ever came here, Peter knew it would be in exactly the same place as the common room in his dorm since all the buildings in the complex were laid out exactly alike.

Peter pulled the shiny, red apple out of his pocket, the one KC had rejected a few minutes ago, and bit into it as he climbed the stairs. *What a stubborn girl she was,* he thought. He knew she'd been dying for something to eat, but she had this silly notion that she needed to lose weight for the photo shoot Wednesday. Didn't she realize that she already looked perfect on camera? Peter had photographed her loads of times, and while he'd never captured her in anything as skimpy as a bathing suit, he knew any photographer's lens would love every detail of her face and body.

Peter knew, too, how much KC had wanted him to hold her, even if she hadn't allowed him to. He could *feel* that she loved him, no matter how businesslike she tried to act around him. It was clear in every restrained little kiss she gave him, in every tight-lipped smile. The only thing Peter couldn't understand was *why* KC felt the need to hold herself back. What was she afraid of? He didn't want anything from her, except to love her without the fear of being rejected. But as long as she continued to keep her feelings hidden, Peter would be forced to do the same.

When Peter entered the common room, he saw that several rows of folding chairs had been set up facing the windows. Stripes of midday sunlight sneaked through the venetian blinds, illuminating swirling dustmotes in the musty air. A tall, well-built, young man in a polo shirt was handing out flyers to about a dozen students sitting in the chairs. Peter recognized Josh Gaffey sitting next to Brooks Baldwin. Peter didn't know either one of them well, but he'd spent a fair amount of time with both since they were each going out with KC's girlfriends.

"Mind if I sit here?" Peter asked as he stood by an empty seat next to Josh.

"Hello Peter. Sit down," Josh said in a friendly tone. "Hey! Are you going on this whitewater rafting trip, too? I didn't know you were the outdoor type."

"I'm not, actually," Peter said as he sat down on the cold metal chair. "But I just bought a waterproof camera, and I thought this might be a good time to try it out. I want to do some studies of water, you know, moving water, still water, spray, foam, etcetera."

"Sounds interesting," Brooks said, leaning forward in his chair, "but it might be hard for you to focus your camera when you've got a paddle in both hands and you're skidding down the rapids at forty miles an hour."

"I'll figure something out," Peter said. "Anyway, I still haven't decided if I'm going or not. I might have to spend some extra time in the darkroom."

The guy in the polo shirt handed Peter a flyer, then perched on a windowsill in front of his audience. "Hi," he said, running his hand along the top of his bristly, blond, brush cut. "I'm Michael Walker, and I'm the senior in charge of the whitewater rafting trip. All the information is on the sheets I gave you, but I'll just go over the basics and answer any questions you might have.

"To start off, it's an all-day trip sponsored by Martin's World of Water. We'll be leaving here at eight-thirty next Saturday morning, and we should be back sometime around five-thirty. You'll need to pack a lunch. The weather should probably be warm enough so that you can wear a swimsuit under shorts and a T-shirt, but if it's cold, Martin's will provide us with wetsuits at no extra charge.

"For those of you who've never gone whitewater

rafting before, all I can tell you is—it's a thrill a minute. The Wahalla River is a Class Three-Four whitewater run with forty-seven quality, named rapids, and a seven-mile stretch of almost continuous, wild, water action. Yes, it's dangerous, but only if you don't follow instructions. You'll each be provided with helmets and life preservers, and there will be a guide in your boat at all times. As long as you do what the guide tells you, you'll have a great time and come back in one piece. Any questions?"

After Michael had explained how to waterproof a lunch (in giant plastic containers provided by Martin's), how to stay in a raft (by hooking your toes under the toe-holds), and where to meet (the bus would be parked in the driveway behind Rapids Hall Saturday morning), the meeting ended.

"Too bad Winnie's not going," Brooks told Josh as they and Peter lingered for a moment in their chairs. "Although it's probably better, in a way. Knowing Winnie, she'd stand up on the edge of the raft and try to balance as it's twisting around in the waves."

"I don't think she'd do anything so crazy," Josh said, "at least, not anymore. Winnie's calmed down a lot lately. She's so stable now I almost don't recognize her. But I'm not complaining."

"Well, my girlfriend's a fearless warrior," Brooks said. "She's brilliant, disciplined, and can run faster than a racehorse. She's also madly in love with me. In fact, don't be surprised if . . ." Brooks abruptly shut his mouth and grinned, his blue eyes gleaming.

"If what?" Josh asked.

"Nothing," Brooks said, crossing his muscular arms over his chest and propping his hiking boots on the chair in front of him. "I don't want to jump the gun. Let's just say Melissa and I are getting along better than ever."

Peter tossed his apple core into a garbage can beneath the window and tried to ignore the envy that was creeping inside his skin. It sounded like Brooks, Josh, and their respective girlfriends were ready to make serious commitments to each other. So what was wrong with KC? Why couldn't she admit her feelings the way her friends did?

Instead of feeling closer to KC, Peter had the uncomfortable suspicion that she was moving further and further away. But it wasn't that there was a problem between them. It was as if KC was moving up to a higher level of accomplishment with her modeling. Granted, she hadn't even gone on her first shoot yet, but Peter was sure she'd be very successful. It wouldn't be long before she'd start getting jobs outside of Springfield, maybe in New York or Paris or Rome.

With all that glamorous globe-hopping, she'd

soon forget about an ordinary amateur photographer like himself. Sure, he was talented, but so far he hadn't done anything more important than projects for school and the Classic Calendar they'd sold on campus last Christmas. That hardly compared to the big bucks KC would soon be earning, not to mention the national recognition.

"Well, guys," Brooks said, standing up and stretching his hands up to the ceiling, "I guess I'll see you bright and early next Saturday morning."

Josh, too, rose from his chair. "It's back to the computer center for me. I've got to get Alphie ready for the Computer Fair Friday night."

"Oh, yeah," said Brooks. "How's that going? It's amazing the way you rigged that robot to recognize people's voices. How'd you do that?"

"I'll explain on the way out," Josh said. "You coming, Peter?"

Peter, who'd barely been listening, shook his head. "I'll catch you later," he said as they walked away.

National recognition. The words were still echoing inside his head. Was that what really bothered him —that KC might become famous and successful while he was stuck up here, in the corner of the country, puttering around in a darkroom that was really nothing more than a converted closet? Or was it that he was afraid that with KC gone, his life would be completely empty?

Either way, he had to do something about this. He couldn't just feel sorry for himself while she went on to bigger and better things. He had to find something to occupy his time—no, more than that. He had to figure out a way to be recognized for his own talents. And he knew exactly where to start.

Last semester, Peter had entered the Morgan Foundation Photo Contest, a prestigious competition sponsored by the Morgan Museum of Photography in New York City. People from all over the world had submitted photographs, hoping to win the grand prize—a four-page feature in *Photography* magazine and a year of free study in Europe. Peter had made the finals, which was quite an honor since only 50 out of 5,000 people got that far. But all he'd gotten was a framed certificate and a letter from the president of the Morgan Foundation. Hardly enough to fill his autobiography, if he ever wrote one.

He had another chance, though, this year. The application deadline was this week, but as a former finalist, all he had to do was call to reactivate his application and send in recent photos. The more Peter thought about it, the clearer it became that this was exactly what he had to do. He owed it to himself. His pictures this year were better than the ones he'd done in high school; he'd been experimenting more with light and shadow and texture. He had a good chance of winning.

Peter jumped up so quickly that the metal folding chair tipped over and crashed into the row of chairs behind it. Quickly righting it, Peter raced across the common room, downstairs, and outside to his motorcycle. He hopped on, buckled his helmet, and gunned the motor. He couldn't wait to get back to Coleridge Hall and start going through his portfolio to find his best photographs.

Even without looking, he knew the first one he would choose. It was a black and white portrait, shot in soft, late afternoon light, of a beautiful girl with high cheekbones, unruly, long hair, and large, gray eyes. Like all his best work, it was a photo of KC.

Seven

The round, white Frisbee flew in a straight line over Winnie's head, then paused against the backdrop of clear, blue sky. It quivered slightly as it rotated, before being speared by an extended index finger. A colorful beachball popped into the air, neatly avoiding a football sailing smoothly in the opposite direction. A red kite in the shape of a bird with a long tail, climbed higher and higher toward the brightly burning sun.

Winnie took in the aerial scene as she lay on the dorm green Sunday afternoon, next to Josh. Josh snoozed peacefully in the grass, his face shaded from the sun with a stack of computer printouts. He'd worked so late last night on his robot for the computer fair that he'd fallen asleep as soon as his head had touched the ground.

Winnie didn't mind, though. She had enough work to do preparing for the Crisis Hotline fundraiser. She'd brought all her lists with her so she could figure out exactly who was doing what. So many people had volunteered to help that her main problem would be making sure everybody had enough to do. This was the first time she'd ever taken on such a major responsibility, and she didn't want to blow it.

"Mmmmph," Josh said, announcing that he had awakened. He rolled over in the grass and flung his arm across Winnie's stomach.

Winnie ran her fingers up and down the inside of Josh's bare arm. It felt so smooth against her fingertips. Using her well-toned abdominal muscles to pull herself up to a sitting position, Winnie raised Josh's hand to her lips and kissed it.

"Hi," Josh murmured groggily. "How long have I been out?"

"Only about five hours," Winnie said in a serious voice. "The groundskeeper wanted to plant you right here, but I talked him out of it."

"Very funny." Josh gathered up his computer papers, which had scattered in the grass. "Guess I didn't get much work done. How about you?"

"Actually," Winnie said, "I've almost figured out

everybody's assignments for the fundraiser. You want to hear how I'm organizing it?"

"Sure." Josh lay down in the grass again and rested his head on Winnie's lap.

"Okay," Winnie said, holding her neatly written notes so Josh could see them. "First I made a diagram with a broad overview of the entertainment portion of the show. We have to fill an hour-and-a-half—that's why I've drawn these little boxes down the side of the page indicating exactly how much time has elapsed at each point in the show. Faith asked Freya to sing some operatic arias for us; some other Coleridge Hall students are going to perform also. I'm just worried that no one will want to pay big bucks to see an amateur show."

"Everyone in Coleridge is talented," Josh said. "But maybe you should try to book a local band."

"I thought of that," Winnie said. "The problem is that the ones I got in touch with all want to be paid."

"Well, don't worry too much. I'm sure the show will be a sellout. Where's it going to be?" Josh asked, twisting the tiny, blue earring in his left ear.

"Swedenborg House. Teresa and David at the hotline used their grad school connections to get it for us. And everybody else I know is helping, too. KC got the Tri Betas to provide decorations and refreshments. Kimberly and her boyfriend Derek have volunteered to usher, and Peter's going to man the T-shirt booth. The only friends who aren't going or helping are Lauren and Melissa. Lauren is working all night at the Springfield Inn, and Melissa is catatonic right now."

"What do you mean?"

Winnie pressed her lips together. She'd almost given away Melissa's secret! Melissa had come back to the room Tuesday night with the strangest look on her face. Her body had been all stiff, too, like someone had dipped her in cement. Winnie practically had to pry out of her that Brooks had proposed! And Winnie had nearly passed out at the news. Brooks—the little boy she'd known since third grade when he was less than four feet tall—the skinny adolescent who was the smartest kid in her eighth grade honors French class —the sturdy, high school soccer star who'd dated her friend Faith for four years. It was hard to believe Brooks was even *old* enough to get married!

On the other hand, Winnie wasn't totally surprised that Brooks thought he was ready for such a big step. Brooks had always been mature for his age. He probably would have proposed to Faith if she hadn't broken up with him when they first got to college.

Meanwhile, Melissa was a nervous wreck. Winnie had never seen her so disjointed. While Melissa was managing to get to class and track practice, she spent the rest of her time pacing in their dorm room or sitting on her bed, staring into space. Winnie was dying to share the news with someone, especially Josh. It wasn't every day you got a juicy piece of gossip like that. But she'd promised Melissa she wouldn't say anything, at least not until Melissa had made up her mind whether or not to say yes.

"Earth to Winnie," Josh said, staring up at her with amused brown eyes.

"Hmmm?" Winnie asked. "What was the question?"

"You said your roommate was catatonic," Josh said with his lopsided grin. "I was just wondering if you'd care to explain."

"Uh, actually, no. I mean, I *would*, but I can't. I mean, maybe I can later, but I can't right now. You know what I mean?"

"I wish I did," Josh said. "Does it have anything to do with Brooks? He was acting a little weird yesterday at the meeting for the whitewater rafting trip."

"We were talking about the hotline fundraiser," Winnie said brightly, trying to change the subject. "I think you're right. A rock singer or comedian would be better. Not too many people are going to be willing to pay twenty dollars to hear Italian arias and see a mime. Most people have more mainstream taste. Now I wish I hadn't volunteered to organize this benefit. It's starting to give me grief."

"Is that the only thing you're worried about?" Josh asked, sitting up and facing Winnie.

"Well, no, of course not. I'm worried that the guy who's Xeroxing the programs won't make enough for everyone who comes, and I'm worried that the lights we're borrowing from the drama department will blow a fuse, and I'm worried . . ."

"I'm not talking about the hotline," Josh said, taking hold of Winnie's hands and searching her eyes with his. "I'm talking about your father."

Winnie avoided Josh's eyes and started shuffling through her notes. "What does he have to do with anything?" she muttered.

"That's exactly my point," Josh said, ducking his head down so she had to look into his eyes again. "You're acting like you never even met him, like seeing him for the first time since you were two made absolutely no difference to you."

"You've got that right," Winnie said, pulling her sneakers over her bare feet and tying them quickly. "I am proud to say that I didn't let him get to me. He tried to be really charming and friendly, but I didn't let my guard down for a minute. Do you realize what a victory that is for me? After eighteen years of getting hyper over nothing, I've learned how to stay calm and keep things in perspective."

Winnie picked up her papers, hopped lightly to her feet, and started across the green toward their dorm.

"You call that perspective?" Josh asked, grabbing his printouts and walking rapidly to keep up with her. "Since when is ignoring the father you haven't seen in sixteen years keeping things in perspective? Haven't you allowed yourself to feel *anything* about this? Are you happy? Sad? Angry? Did he feel like your father or a complete stranger? Did you have anything in common?"

"I don't want to hear this," Winnie cried, trying to cover her ears with her papers as she half-ran toward Forest Hall.

"But you have to face it eventually," Josh said, grabbing her shoulders and making her face him. "Whether or not you want to acknowledge it, your father's back and he wants to get to know you. Are you just going to pretend he doesn't exist? Have you even stopped to consider how *he* feels?"

"What he feels doesn't matter," Winnie said, her breath coming in shaky gasps. "Byron told me that himself. It's what *I* feel that's important, and what I feel right now is that I want peace. I want quiet. I don't want to be the Winnie who's always on the verge of freaking out. I want to feel nothing."

"Oh, great," Josh snapped angrily. "You really have made progress. You've gone from being a girl who gets excited about things, who's bubbly and enthusiastic and fun, to someone who's afraid to be human. Sure, it's scary facing your father again after all these years, but are you going to let this opportunity slip through your fingers just because you're afraid? Is that the price you're willing to pay just to have some calm in your life?"

"You don't understand," Winnie began, but Josh interrupted her.

"I understand perfectly," he said. "You've lost sixteen years of being with your father, and if you don't do something right now, you might lose him for the rest of your life. Please, Winnie," he urged, gripping her arms so tightly it hurt. "Don't cut yourself off. Don't become some cold, remote ice cube. Be the Winnie that I love, the Winnie who takes chances and plunges into things headfirst."

Josh's words hit home. Winnie's whole body was trembling. She'd been doing her utmost to control her emotions—trying to pretend that her father had never called, that she hadn't seen him, that he still didn't exist. She had tried to create a false sense of calm. But ever since she'd met him, she'd had a constant headache and bad dreams every night. And every day, she'd made some excuse to walk past Mill Pond with the crazy notion that he'd be sitting on the bench where she'd met him.

Maybe Josh was right. Maybe deep down, she

really did want to get to know him a little better, or at least listen to the rest of his explanation. If she didn't, she might regret it as long as she lived.

"Okay," Winnie finally said in a barely audible voice. "I'll call him. I know I'm going to regret it, but I'll give him another chance."

Eight

A sound arose in the gymnasium like a crack of thunder, like a giant tidal wave breaking against a rocky shore. The U. of S. volleyball team had won its fifteenth straight victory.

Lauren crumpled up the sheet of notebook paper she'd been writing on and tossed it into the wastebasket next to Faith's desk. So far her article didn't sound like a sports story, it sounded like bad fiction. And without any quotes from the players or the coach, even starting over wasn't going to make it much better. Lauren wanted to kick herself for being such a chicken at the volleyball game. If only she'd had the nerve to go into the men's locker room, she might have handed in her story by now.

Instead, here she was in Faith's room, avoiding her dismal apartment, and trying to make up facts about a game she'd only half-watched.

She needed to find an angle. Maybe student reaction to the U. of S. winning streak was the answer. She had lots of quotes she'd jotted down during the game.

"Amazing! Absolutely incredible!"

"They're hot! This is definitely going to go down in the history books!"

Lauren wanted to gag. This approach sounded like a commercial on late-night television for a Jiffy-Matic dicer-slicer-potato peeler-hedge trimmer. Covering the men's volleyball team was turning out to be a disaster! The editors at the *Weekly Journal* didn't expect Lauren to turn in an article, since no one even knew she was writing one. It had become more a matter of principle. It wasn't fair that the men's teams didn't have a reception area for reporters, when the women's teams did.

Lauren had to admit to herself, though, that she could have gone into the men's locker room. No one had denied her access. It was no one's fault but her own that she didn't have enough material for an article. Lauren sighed and lay her head on her blank notebook.

"When I hear the music, it does something to me," sang a loud, off-key voice outside the door.

Lauren heard a key turning in the lock. The door opened and Liza appeared, lugging a heavy totebag dripping with dirty tights, tap shoes, sheet music, and a bathing cap with floppy rubber daisies. Her curly, orange hair sprung from her head, and her pale face seemed even paler in contrast to her bright, red lipstick. She wore a blue velvet porkpie hat which didn't match the floral print bodysuit she wore under a chiffon overshirt. On her feet, she wore shiny silver cowboy boots with extra-high heels.

"What are you doing here?" Liza asked in a friendly tone. "Are you moving back in?"

Lauren, in an effort to save money, had sold her dorm contract to Liza a few weeks earlier, so Liza was Faith's new roommate. Lauren knew the rooming situation hadn't worked out too well for Faith. In fact, it was awful—Faith couldn't stand Liza. That's why Faith had invited Lauren to spend as much time as she wanted in her old room in Coleridge Hall—Faith wanted Lauren there as a buffer zone, but of course Lauren couldn't tell Liza that.

"I . . . uh . . . needed to work on an article, so Faith said I could work at her desk since my apartment's so far away. I don't want to bother you, though. I can study in the library just as easily." Lauren shut her notebook, dropped it in her knapsack, and stood up to go.

"Don't be silly!" Liza said. "Siddown! Make yourself at home! Mi room, su room. That's Spanish, sort of." Liza pushed Lauren back down into the desk chair. "What are you working on?" she asked, sitting down on Faith's desk.

"It's nothing you'd be interested in," Lauren said quietly.

"I'm interested in *everything!*" Liza declared, "and if you don't tell me, I'll make you play twenty questions with me until I guess what it is. And if I don't get it in twenty, I'll just keep guessing, so you might as well tell me now."

Lauren laughed, despite her discomfort. "It's an article on the men's volleyball team for the *Journal*. At least, it's supposed to be, but I haven't written anything yet, and at the rate I'm going, it looks like I never will."

"Why not?" Liza asked, taking off her blue velvet hat and crossing the room to hang it on the wall among a dozen other hats. It was quite a collection. Some had veils, some had plastic fruit, one was a fake-fur pillbox with a little stuffed bird sitting on top. There was even a Mexican sombrero with the words "Have a Nice Day" woven into the brim. Liza pulled off her cowboy boots and lined them up between her purple hightop sneakers and platform sandals. Then she stepped into a pair of fuzzy pink bunny slippers and sat down on her bed.

"Do you really want to know why?" Lauren asked. Though Lauren hadn't spoken of this to anyone, even Dash or Faith, she felt she could talk to Liza. Maybe it was because she didn't know Liza well enough to be worried about what she would think of her. Or maybe it was because Liza was so off-the-wall, nothing could faze her. "I'll tell you why," Lauren said, resting her forearms on the back of her chair. "It's because I'm a wimp. I'm a spineless jellyfish who doesn't have the guts to stand up for myself."

Liza's bushy brown eyebrows shot up with interest. "Please continue," she said. "This sounds absolutely fascinating, so don't leave out a word." She crossed one pudgy leg over the other and pushed her mass of curls behind her ears so she could hear better.

Lauren explained what had happened after the volleyball game. "I just stood there like a coward while Charlie Mandelkern barged into the locker room like he owned the place. And now here it is, four days after the game, and I have yet to put a single word on paper. It's really because I have nothing to say. I tried calling the captain of the team to arrange an interview, but he said he didn't have any time to talk to me. He's got *real* reporters from local TV stations and national newspapers taking up all his time, so what does he need me for?"

"Maybe one of your editors can call him," Liza suggested. "You know, use a little pull to get you the interview. That's how things are done. It's all pull and connections."

"I did think of that," Lauren admitted, "and I wanted to talk to my boyfriend Dash about it since he's an assistant editor at the *Journal*. But Dash has measles. Can you believe it? At his age? I never had them when I was younger, so I can't go near him."

"Doesn't he have a phone?" Liza asked.

Lauren shook her head. "He's not antisocial, he just doesn't want to pay a phone bill. The only contact I've had with him is when I drop off care packages in front of his apartment door. So much for connections. It's probably too late for a general story anyway, and I certainly can't offer any deep insights when I haven't interviewed any of the players. I guess I deserve this for being such a scaredy-cat."

Liza shook her head. "I can't believe you're talking this way," she said. "Have you heard all the words you've used? Coward. Wimp. Scaredy-cat. Is that what you want to be a writer for? So you won't need a thesaurus when you want to insult yourself? You're your own worst enemy!"

Lauren reeled back from the violence of Liza's reaction. She certainly hadn't expected this. Now she was sorry for opening her mouth. She should have believed it when Faith told her what a loudmouth Liza was.

"Look," Lauren said, rising unsteadily to her feet, "I really should be going."

"No!" Liza declared, jumping up also, and taking hasty, mincing steps across the room in her bunny slippers. "You're not leaving until we solve this problem."

"We?" Lauren asked, wishing there was some way to shield herself from the intensity in Liza's blue eyes. What had she gotten herself into?

"Yes, we," Liza said, hefting her heavy shoulder bag up to Faith's desk. "I've already figured out step one of our plan."

Lauren sank weakly into Faith's desk chair. She felt as trapped as if Liza had tied her there with rope. Liza rooted through her bag, flinging tapshoes, tights, and makeup on the floor. As Lauren watched helplessly, her stomach began to twist itself into a knot. She was beginning to understand how much Faith must be suffering with Liza for a roommate. And it was all Lauren's fault for putting Faith in that position. Lauren was surprised Faith would even talk to her anymore.

"Aha!" Liza exclaimed, pulling out a wrinkled, dirty copy of that week's *Journal.* "Now, I know there's a calendar of sports events in here somewhere."

Liza flipped to the last page of the newspaper and scanned it with laser-beam eyes, then looked up at Lauren, her face beaming with triumph.

"I *knew* it!" Liza said. "I thought I saw it this morning. This is Monday, right? The volleyball team's having another match this afternoon against Cascadia College. In fact . . ." Liza consulted an antique silver pocket watch that she wore on a chain around her neck, "the game started fifteen minutes ago. If we get over there now, you should be in time to interview the players."

"No, I don't think . . ." Lauren started to protest, but Liza pulled her to her feet and shoved her knapsack at her.

"Just give me a minute to get my shoes on," Liza said, kicking off her slippers and quickly tying on her purple hightop sneakers. "I'm trying to get out of the habit of wearing heels," Liza explained. "They're just no good for your feet, even though the line is much more flattering." Liza jumped up again and grabbed Lauren's arm with pincer-like fingers. "Here we go!" she said cheerfully, pushing Lauren out of the room ahead of her.

Liza marched Lauren down the hall past a line of girls in Lycra shorts and midriff tops who were practicing an energetic dance routine to rap music.

"Look, Liza," Lauren tried to reason with her,

"it's nice of you to take an interest in my problem, but I really don't think it's necessary."

"Of course it's necessary," Liza said as she pulled Lauren down the stairs and out the door of Coleridge Hall. "We have to strike a blow for womankind. Besides, if the team wins today, you'll have an even better story than last time, because it'll be one more victory in their winning streak."

Lauren couldn't argue with that. She also couldn't pry her arm loose from Liza's grip, so she stopped trying. She and Liza walked quickly across the green, through McLaren Plaza, past the medical school, and over the broad field leading to the gymnasium/stadium complex.

"The game will be over soon," Lauren started to say as Liza pulled open the back door to the gymnasium. Her voice was drowned out by a mighty roar. It was the U. of S. crowd going nuts as the men's volleyball team won another point.

"What's the score?" Liza asked, pulling on the sleeve of a young woman with short, dark hair.

"Fourteen-zero," the woman said excitedly. "They're going for their eleventh shut-out, sixteenth straight victory. You see that guy over there?" she asked, pointing to a well-dressed young man speaking into a microphone before a video camera. "He's from KPOR! They came all the way from the capitol to cover this. This is big news!"

"Oh, I know!" Liza said. "I know all about it. My friend here is writing a feature on it for a very important publication."

The woman started to smile at Lauren, but everyone's attention was suddenly called back to the volleyball court. The U. of S. server, a hulking six-footer with powerful arms, was poised to pop the ball across the net. Though the gym was packed with people, the huge hall was absolutely quiet, as if no one dared even to breathe. Calmly, confidently, the server pulled back his arm. Without taking her eyes off him, Lauren rummaged around in her knapsack for her notebook.

The server's fist snapped forward against the ball with such force that it sounded like a shot being fired. The Cascadia team, in navy and white, was ready, and valiantly tried to keep the ball in the air, managing to send it back to the Springfield side. The ball was high, though, and soft. The center player on Springfield's front line leaped high into the air and spiked it back over the net. He slammed it to the ground so hard that the ball split open on the shiny wooden floor.

For a second, there was no sound but the hiss of the ball as it slowly deflated. Then there was the deafening noise of cheers, screams, stamping feet, applause, and nasal-sounding horns like the kind blown at New Year's parties. Joyful bodies rushed down the bleachers onto the floor of the gymnasium. Lauren cowered against the back wall of the gym, afraid she'd be trampled.

"Come on," Liza said, pulling her into the thick of the crowd. "Now's our chance. Show me where the men's locker room is."

Lauren didn't try to protest. They weren't far from the door in the side wall marked "Men." Towering hunks in sweatsoaked purple nylon were already muscling their way through the crowd and pushing through the swinging door.

"Is this it?" Liza asked.

Lauren nodded. "But I don't think we should . . ."

Liza grabbed Lauren's arm again and pulled her through the swinging door. Parallel banks of gray, metal lockers ran the length of the large room, with long, wooden benches in the center of the aisles between them. A row of sinks was attached to the wall with the door. At the end of the row of sinks was another doorway leading to an open shower stall. There were no shower curtains, and Lauren could hear water running in a corner of the tiled stall she couldn't see. That meant a guy was taking a shower, and if she moved slightly to the left or right, she could probably see him!

"Let's get out of here," Lauren said nervously.

"Not on your life," Liza answered, as she

marched further into the locker room, her head swiveling as she looked around with bright interest. "You wanted to get in, you're in. Now all we have to do is interview some of the players."

The door behind Lauren kept swinging open and closed as more and more players entered. There was the clang of metal lockers being thrown open. Several well-muscled men, clad only in white towels wrapped around their waists, padded toward the showers in bare feet.

"*Please, Liza,*" Lauren begged. "I'm *so embarrassed!*"

"Loosen up," Liza said. She pulled Lauren up to a tall, handsome, bare-chested guy who'd emerged from the shower. His dark, wet hair was slicked straight back and his skin still glistened with tiny droplets of water. "Excuse me," Liza said, tapping his bare shoulder with a long red fingernail. "My friend here, is covering your *phenomenal* volleyball playing for the *Journal,* and she was wondering if you could give her your perspective on your winning streak."

"Sure," the guy said, his brown eyes friendly. "What would you like to know?"

Lauren hesitated for a second longer. Could she really interview a man who was barely dressed? On the other hand, if she didn't, she might as well forget about ever covering another men's sporting event. So much for standing up for her gender.

"Uh . . . hi," Lauren said faintly, flipping open her notebook and unhooking the pen she'd clipped to it. "I'm Lauren Turnbell-Smythe. You are . . ."

"Larry Greenberg."

Lauren quickly jotted down his name. "I've done a little research on the team and learned that most of this year's players are the same people who played last year when the team had an undistinguished re-cord. You also had the same coach. What do you think made the difference this year?"

"That's a good question," Larry said, drying his hair with a second towel that had been draped around his shoulders. "I'd have to say it was a change in attitude. We really didn't play up to our potential last year, and I think every one of us real-ized that. When we started practicing this year, we all just sort of decided it was do or die. And after we won the first couple of games, it started to build."

"I see," Lauren said. Liza gave her a wink, and Lauren felt her body relax a little. This wasn't as difficult as she'd thought. "Has the team trained any differently this year? Are you practicing harder or longer?"

"Not longer," Larry said, "but we *are* cross-train-ing more. Last year we spent almost all our time playing volleyball. This year we're also running and working out with weights, and I think both of those things have helped."

A tanned young man with long, blond hair and sharply defined muscles appeared behind Larry. He was wearing only a pair of baggy boxer shorts. "Coach Brandes also made us read a book called *Brain Power: Winning's All in Your Head,*" the blond guy added. "That helped a lot, too. There's this quote in the book that you're supposed to re-peat over and over to yourself before a game."

"I think I can win. I know I can win. I think I can win. I know I can win," Larry and the blond guy repeated over and over again, pumping their fists. Male voices from all over the locker room chimed in.

"This is great!" Lauren whispered to Liza. "This is all stuff I can use."

"Excuse me!" said a loud, deep voice that drowned out the chanting of the players.

Lauren turned and saw a middle-aged man with a protruding gut and a purple nylon windbreaker enter from the gym. Embroidered on the front of his jacket in white thread was the name Brandes.

"What do you two young ladies think you're do-ing here?" Coach Brandes demanded. "Don't you know this is the men's locker room?"

"I'm covering the story for the *Weekly Journal,*"

Lauren announced, feeling bolstered by Liza's presence and the success of her interview.

"Not in my locker room you're not," the coach said, grabbing Lauren's and Liza's arms and pushing them toward the locker room door.

"You can't kick us out," Lauren said. "That's sex discrimination!"

"We'll sue!" Liza threatened.

"Have your lawyer call my lawyer," the coach laughed as he shooed them out the door.

"What a male chauvinist pig," Liza said, sticking her tongue out at the door. "We should take this to the University Board of Governors."

"We should definitely do something," Lauren agreed. "But at least I have enough for a story. I think I'll call it 'Mind over Muscle.'"

"That's good!" Liza grinned. "Very catchy."

"I can't thank you enough, Liza," Lauren said. "I wish I had your guts."

"It's sort of like that book the players read," Liza explained. "If you think positive, you can do anything you set your mind to. You just can't let yourself be afraid."

"That's easier said than done. I'm always worried I'll offend someone."

"*You?*" Liza laughed. "You're so polite, I'll bet you don't even know how to raise your voice."

"That's probably true," Lauren admitted. "Hey, I

know. How'd you like to be my personal trainer? You can come over once a week and teach me how to assert myself."

"It's a deal," Liza said, extending her hand.

Lauren shook it. "Meanwhile, do you have any plans for dinner? They're serving five-alarm chili in the dining commons; I hear the fire department's set up emergency hoses at every table."

"Sounds great!" Liza said, flashing her thousand-watt grin.

Nine

....

"**A**ren't you ready yet?" Josh asked, poking his head inside Winnie's room. "It's almost seven o'clock. We'll never make it to the restaurant on time at this rate."

"Let him wait," Winnie said, standing amid a pile of rejected outfits she'd tossed on the floor. "After sixteen years, a few more minutes shouldn't make a difference."

"Is that what you're wearing to meet your father?" Josh asked, noting Winnie's choice of a black T-shirt, black jeans, and plain, white canvas sneakers. "It's not very festive."

Winnie shrugged as she pulled a faded denim jacket off its wire hanger in her closet. "We're not exactly going to Mardi Gras," she said. "Well, if we're going, let's go."

Winnie and Josh left Forest Hall and headed out into the starry night.

"You're in a great mood," Josh remarked sarcastically as they took a short-cut across the green. "I hope you're not going to act this way with your father."

Winnie knew she was behaving badly, but for some reason she couldn't stop herself. Maybe it was because having agreed to meet her father again, she felt exposed and vulnerable. Now her father would probably think that she liked him, and he'd try to get closer to her. It didn't help that Josh was on her father's side.

"Just be glad I'm going at all," Winnie said sullenly. "It's more than he deserves."

They crossed Main Street and cut through a maze of alleyways. Emerging onto a side street, they reached a squat, brick building with ancient, crusted, plateglass windows. A faded wooden sign over the door read Hondo's Cafe. Hondo's, home of the foot-long, submarine sandwich, was U. of S.'s oldest and most popular hangout.

Winnie and Josh entered the brightly lit restaurant. The walls were lined with pennants and yellowing photographs of sports teams from Springfield's past. Sawdust covered the floor and the air was filled with happy chatter and vintage rock music from an old jukebox.

"Is that him?" Josh asked, pointing to a booth near the wooden counter where people stood on line to order.

Winnie glanced over to where Josh was pointing. Byron Jennings sat alone, nervously adjusting his wide, bright, red tie with yellow slashes running through it. He wore a crisp, white shirt and a black-and-white houndstooth jacket. His slightly thinning, dark hair was slicked straight back and his brown eyes flitted anxiously around the restaurant.

"Yes, that's him," Winnie said, taking a step back.

Byron spotted them and was instantly on his feet. "Hi, Winnie," he said, rushing to greet them. He leaned forward to kiss Winnie's cheek.

"Byron," Winnie said coldly. "This is my boyfriend, Josh Gaffey."

"Pleased to meet you," Byron said, vigorously shaking Josh's hand. "Come sit down. What would you like to eat? Anything you want, it's on me." Winnie ordered a meatball parmigiana submarine and Josh ordered an Italian sub with french fries. "I'll be right back," Byron promised, scurrying to the counter to place their order.

"See," Josh said to Winnie as they sat next to each other on the wooden bench. "He's not so bad."

"Buying a couple of subs after never paying child support is hardly grounds for forgiveness," Winnie said sourly. "After everything my mother told me about him, he's lucky I'm even talking to him."

"Did you call your mother and tell her you heard from him?" Josh asked.

"Actually," Winnie said, "I haven't spoken to my mother yet. I figured it wasn't important enough to bother her with." Winnie ignored Josh as he rolled his eyes. "She's never described him in a particularly flattering way, you know."

"What way is that?"

"Lowlife. Infantile. Irresponsible. Flattering words like that."

"Maybe that's just her side of the story," Josh suggested. "Maybe she was really hurt by the divorce. Didn't you tell me once that he left her for another woman? That could explain why she's so bitter."

"Bon appetit, *mes amis!*" Byron said, bursting in on their conversation. He balanced a plastic tray loaded with food on one hand, and twirled an imaginary handlebar moustache with the other. "We 'ave 'ere ze very delectable meatball sub *avec fromage,*" he said in a convincing French accent, handing Winnie her meatball sub. "And, also, for ze gentleman, ze sub Italien, *avec les pommes frites!*" Byron unloaded Josh's plate along with two sodas in huge glasses that looked like fishbowls. He sat down across from Winnie and Josh, his own place empty.

"Aren't you eating anything?" Josh asked.

Byron shrugged. "I ate at the hotel," he said. "I'm really here to see Winnie, not to eat, although I will take a french fry." He leaned forward and grabbed a fat, greasy fry.

"So," Josh said, looking from Winnie to Byron. "I guess you guys have a lot to talk about."

Winnie didn't bother to look up at Josh or her father. She just swirled her sub's melted cheese and tomato sauce with a plastic fork. She had nothing to say to her father, anyway. If he wanted to talk, it was up to him to say something.

"What brings you to town, Mr. Jennings?" Josh tried again.

"Call me Byron," Winnie's father said, plucking another french fry from Josh's paper container and munching while he talked. "Actually, Winnie is what brings me to town. I guess she told you that I haven't exactly been part of her life, so I understand completely why she'd rather look at tomato sauce than my ugly mug. I'm just grateful she's given me another chance to explain myself, although I have this feeling that you had something to do with it. I'm right, aren't I? You brought her here."

"Well . . ." Josh hemmed and hawed. "I didn't really."

"You're a sensitive young man, Josh," Byron said. "You've got heart. I can already see what Winnie sees in you. Hey, I know! I'll tell *you* my sob story, and if you buy any of it maybe you can put in a good word for me."

Josh laughed. "I'm willing to listen," he said, "and even if your adorable daughter *acts* like she's not, I'll bet she's listening, too."

Winnie wanted to puke. Josh and her father had just met, and they were already acting like old friends.

Byron took a deep breath. "Okay," he said. "If I leave anything out, just ask Winnie to fill you in later tonight when she's yelling at you for being nice to me. Winnie's mother and I divorced when Winnie was two. It was . . . well . . . messy to put it mildly. But the thing I always wanted Winnie to understand was that I didn't divorce *her*. I wanted to see her, spend time with her, be a dad to her, but her mother wouldn't let me anywhere near her. Part of the divorce settlement was that Francine had full custody, and no matter how many times I called, she wouldn't even let me come for a visit."

Fragments of late-night conversations Winnie hadn't even remembered she'd heard suddenly came back to her. *Byron, I said no! It's for her own good, and you know what I'm talking about. . . . It isn't fair to raise her hopes that way. You'll just disappoint her. . . . For the last time, no!* Winnie couldn't have been more than four or five years old when she'd heard her mother's muffled voice from the living room at an hour when she should have been asleep. The calls had stopped after that.

"Not that I blame Francine one bit," Byron continued, drumming his fingers on the table. "I remarried very soon after the divorce and I'm sure she resented me for that. I moved to Denver and started my own business which was quite successful. I wanted to send money for Winnie, but Francine didn't want anything to do with me. My new wife, too, was very possessive and wanted me all to herself, so that made it even harder for me to be with my daughter. After a few more years went by, I finally stopped trying. Maybe I should never have given up, I don't know."

"It sounds like you tried pretty hard," Josh said, opening his mouth wide to get it around his tall sandwich.

Winnie bit the end of her straw. Why hadn't her mother mentioned any of this? When Winnie had asked where her father was, all her mother had said was that she'd be better off not knowing. Didn't she think Winnie would have wanted to know that her father was trying to get in touch with her?

On the other hand, Winnie trusted her mother's

judgment. If her mother had tried that hard to prevent her from seeing her father, she must have had a good reason. The only problem was, Winnie couldn't see what that reason was. All she could see, so far, was a guy who was trying very hard to make her like him.

"There's one thing I don't understand," Josh said, washing down his sub with a sip of cola. "Why now? Why did you come looking for Winnie after all these years?"

Winnie was beginning to feel grateful to Josh for asking all these questions. She really *was* curious to know more, even if she didn't want her father to know that.

Byron sighed and leaned back against the dark wooden bench. "I'm a two-time loser," he said. "My second marriage just ended, too. I won't even go into that. You might say I'm at a juncture in my life. Winnie's the only family I've got. And I knew she would be eighteen. She's legally an adult and can make her own decision whether or not she wants to know me."

That was exactly what Winnie had just been thinking. The more she reflected on what her mother had done, the angrier she became. It really wasn't fair that her mother had denied her an opportunity to know the only father she'd ever have. Even if her father was as bad as her mother said, didn't Winnie have the right to draw her own conclusions?

"Can we please stop talking about me in the third person?" Winnie demanded, finally looking up and catching her father's eye.

"She speaks!" Byron declared happily, doing a little tap dance under the table.

"I knew she'd come around," Josh said, wrapping his arm around Winnie's shoulder and squeezing her.

"Does this mean I'm forgiven?" Byron asked, his face filled with hope.

Winnie shook her head. "Let's just say I'm willing to listen. I mean, I *have* listened. I've heard what you've said. And I do want to make my own decision about you."

"Hooray!" Byron shouted, leaning all the way across the table to pat Winnie's spiky, brown hair. "You know, ever since I met you the other day, I've been dying to do that. Does your hair spike that way naturally? Or do you do something to it?"

Winnie fought hard not to laugh. "It's more or less natural," she said. "I keep trying to grow it so it will eventually hang down instead of sticking straight up, but for some reason my hair won't grow any longer. It's just stubborn, I guess."

"Try axle grease," Byron said, patting his own, slicked back hair. "That's the only way I could ever make mine lie flat." He grinned wide, and Winnie saw her own face smiling at her.

She sighed and felt a lot of the tension leave her body. For the first time in days, she was having a good time. Winnie grinned back at her father, then took a huge bite of her meatball sub. The sandwich was cold and the cheese had congealed, but it tasted delicious.

"That's a girl," Byron said, watching her eat. "I knew you could put it away. I used to watch you inhale jars of baby food, two, three, four at a time. It was amazing to watch."

"Da-a-a-a-ad!" Winnie complained, embarrassed.

Byron's entire face lit up as if he were a Christmas tree that had just been plugged in. Winnie didn't need to ask what he was so happy about. It wasn't until after she'd said the word that she realized what she'd said. But it hadn't felt wrong to say it.

"I've got a great idea," Byron said. "After you're done with that monstrosity of a sandwich, why don't we paint the town? Red, green, yellow, any color you want. Actually, I know exactly where I want to take you."

"Where?" Josh asked, finishing the last bite of his sub.

"It's a surprise," Byron said mysteriously. "But I promise you—it will be a magical experience."

Half an hour later, Winnie, Byron, and Josh

stepped out of a cab on the Strand, Springfield's street of posh boutiques and chic restaurants. A large crowd on the sidewalk was held back from a plain, black door by a velvet rope. Two massive men in leather jackets stood behind the ropes, each holding a clipboard.

"Jean-Michel," a woman called from deep inside the crowd. She waved her well-manicured fingers at one of the leather-jacketed men.

Jean-Michel gave the woman a quick glance, then looked away as if he'd never seen her.

"We're on the guest list!" the manicured woman insisted. "Johannes."

Jean-Michel scanned his clipboard. "Sorry," he said. "I don't see your name."

"Come on, man," a bearded man shouted. "You have to let *somebody* in. How does this place make money if you make everyone stand outside?"

"It's a private party," Jean-Michel said coolly.

"What are we doing here?" Winnie asked her father.

"This is the hottest club in the northwest," her father answered.

"We know," Josh said. "But U. of S. students hardly ever get in. Anyway, the guy said it's a private party."

"That's what they always say," Byron said with a wink. "Just follow me." He began to push his way to the front of the crowd to the annoyance of the people who'd been standing there.

"Who does he think he is?" someone muttered as Winnie struggled to stay close to him.

"John," Byron said to Jean-Michel. The ponytailed man looked at Byron and raised one eyebrow. "I know *we're* on your list," Byron said with a wink. "What happened to Harry, anyway? Did he get sick of Denver?"

Jean-Michel gave the other man a nod, and the velvet rope was opened to admit Winnie, her father, and Josh. A young couple tried to push in behind them, but they were body-blocked by Jean-Michel. The other bodyguard held open the black door for them.

"Enjoy your evening," he said politely.

"I still don't get it," Winnie whispered to her father as the three of them entered a long, dark hallway. "How did we get in when everyone else had to wait outside?"

"I've known John—Jean-Michel—for years," her father said. "He used to work a club in Denver owned by a friend of mine. But that's not important. I just want you to see this place."

A loud, thumping bass line grew louder and louder as they approached a pair of red double doors, surrounded by neon swirls in the shapes of rabbits and birds. Just as Winnie was beginning to wonder where the doorknobs were, the doors flew open and they were engulfed by the loud dance music. Bodies gyrated on the large dance floor, while more neon lights blinked overhead. In the center of the floor was a round, black bar in the shape of an upside down top hat. It looked like the bartenders were standing inside the hat and customers were leaning on the underside of the brim.

At the far end, was an old-fashioned stage with red velvet curtains. The curtains were open to reveal an elderly magician, with a buxom young assistant in a sequinned leotard. The magician was pulling birds, rabbits, and colorful scarves out of a top hat. Several dozen people stood beneath the stage watching, while everyone else around them danced to the throbbing beat.

"Is this great or what?!" Byron shouted over the music. "It's called 'The Magic Act.' It opened three weeks ago, but already people are coming from three states trying to get in!"

"I guess it pays to know people," Winnie said, impressed. "This is really phenomenal!"

"Wait 'til you see the old guy saw the girl in half," Byron said. "He does it in time to Disco Duck. It's so campy, but that's what makes it great."

"Hey," Winnie said to Josh, "I wonder if that magician would be willing to perform at our benefit

Saturday. I'll bet he'd draw a lot bigger audience than what I have planned."

"What benefit?" Byron asked, leading them up a half flight of stairs to a darkened lounge area with overstuffed sofas. The music wasn't as loud there, so they could talk without yelling.

"It's for the Crisis Hotline," Winnie explained. "We're operating on a frayed shoestring right now. In other words, we're broke. I'm helping to organize a benefit to raise money, but so far our entertainment is, well, less than I'd hoped for."

"What were you hoping for?" Byron asked.

Winnie plopped down on a sofa, and her father and Josh sat down on either side of her. "I don't know," Winnie said. "Something more—fun, like a rock singer or a comedian."

"Hmmmm . . ." Byron tapped his chin with an index finger. "I think I might be able to help."

"You?" Winnie asked. "Don't tell me you tell jokes in your spare time."

Byron laughed. "*I* don't, but I know someone who does. Well, actually, he does it for a living. You might have heard of him—Karl Fanfield. He's been on Carson and Letterman a couple of times."

"You know *Karl Fanfield?*" Winnie said, unable to believe her luck. "Didn't he just have his own special on HBO?"

Byron shrugged. "Probably."

"And you think you can get him for Winnie's benefit?" Josh asked, stunned and impressed.

"Let me just make a phone call," Byron said. "I'll be right back."

"Wow!" Josh said, giving Winnie an excited hug. "Your dad is great! Aren't you glad that I talked you into meeting him again?"

"I'm not sorry," Winnie admitted. "Maybe I was too quick to go along with my mother's opinion."

"People change, too," Josh added. "Maybe your father's grown up since he married your mother. He certainly seems nice to me."

Byron reappeared, beaming, a few minutes later. "It's a done deal," he said, joining them on the couch. "I just spoke to Karl's manager, and Karl's available Saturday night. Since Karl's based in Denver, it's an easy trip for him to get here."

"He knows it's a benefit, though, right?" Winnie asked. "We can't pay him anything."

"Not a problem," Byron said confidently. "He's doing it as a favor to me, and I will personally cover his expenses."

"Unbelievable!" Winnie crowed, kicking her legs in the air. "My father got Karl Fanfield to perform free! Wait 'til Teresa and David hear about this! Everyone in Springfield's going to be fighting for tickets. Maybe we can even raise the price!" Winnie threw her arms around him and kissed him on the cheek.

Byron smiled. "Don't thank me. It's the least I could do after all this time."

A few hours later, when Byron dropped off Winnie and Josh at Forest Hall, Winnie felt like she could fly up the stairs to her room. "This was the most fantastic evening of my life!" she rejoiced as they entered the lobby. "If it weren't for you, I never would have given my father another chance. And look how well it's turning out!"

"Glad I could help," Josh said modestly.

"Oh, Josh," Winnie said, wrapping her arms around him and gazing tenderly into his eyes. "You don't realize how much you've done for me. It's not just that Byron got us a star like Karl Fanfield for the benefit. You've given my father back to me. You were absolutely right. I did close myself off before, but I'll never do that again. A whole new part of my life is opening up now—a whole new part of me— and I owe it all to you."

Ten

··············

Melissa stared at her open books. She'd never had so much trouble tuning out the world and concentrating on her studies before. It wasn't that any of her pre-med classes were overwhelming her, it was just that Melissa hadn't been able to decide on *anything* since Brooks had proposed almost a week ago.

Every morning in the dining commons, she'd stared at the selections of oatmeal, eggs, and cold cereal, unable to make up her mind. Often, she hadn't even eaten and she'd already dropped five pounds. Her coach, Terry, was worried about her and had warned her to gain back the weight or he'd force feed her himself.

Melissa had tried to eat, but it was such an effort. Just getting out of bed every morning was an effort. She lay down on a pile of clothes and closed her eyes. Maybe if she just rested for a minute, she'd have enough energy to attack her life again.

"Hear ye, hear ye," Winnie's cheerful voice wafted in through the open doorway. "Come one, come all, to a weekend extravaganza of technology and laughs. Yes, folks, it's a double bill—the Friday night Computer Fair in the new computer building, right here on campus . . ."

". . . and the Saturday spectacular, starring Karl Fanfield. Yes, you heard right, Karl Fanfield is appearing live at Swedenborg House, in honor of the Crisis Hotline benefit," Josh called out. "Buy your tickets now, 'cause they're going fast!"

Melissa opened her eyes and saw Winnie and Josh rushing up and down the hallway. They paused at each door to tape up a flyer with bold black lettering.

"You like it?" Winnie asked, entering the room and fluttering a flyer in front of Melissa's eyes. Winnie's hair, for once, lay flat against her head instead of standing up in little spikes. She wore bright red bicycle shorts, a tight yellow T-shirt, black suspenders, and her orange and black tiger-striped socks. "Josh designed this with a graphics program on his computer. We decided to do a joint advertisement."

Melissa propped herself up on one elbow to read it. "Very nice," she said.

"I know *you're* coming," Winnie said. "Not only will you get to see Karl Fanfield who, by the way, just won a starring role on a new NBC sitcom, but you'll also get to meet my father! He's such a great guy, Melissa. I can't wait to introduce you to him."

"I'll be looking forward to it," Melissa said, managing a smile. "Though with all this advertising you're doing, I'll be lucky to get a seat."

"I'll save one for you," Winnie said with a wink and a grin. "It pays to have connections, if you know what I mean."

"Thanks," Melissa said, lying down and closing her eyes again.

"Hey," Winnie said. "Are you okay? I mean, I know what you're going through right now, but don't you think you'd feel better if you came to some sort of decision?"

Melissa's eyes snapped open. "Of course I would," she said irritably. "That's my whole problem."

Winnie sighed and patted her shoulder. "I want to talk to you about this later," she said. "I'll come back in a little while for an update. Josh!" she called as she careened out of the room, bumping her shoulder against the doorjamb.

Melissa envied Winnie her newfound happiness.

It must be nice to have all the pieces of your life falling into place, she thought, thinking she had had that too—until Brooks had popped the big question.

"Mind if I come in?" Brooks stood in the doorway in his brown-and-white striped rugby shirt and khaki pants. His blond curls lent softness to the square line of his jaw, and his blue eyes looked peaceful beneath their blond lashes.

How could he be so calm at a time like this? Doesn't he realize he's turned my life completely upside down? If it had been anybody else, Melissa would have laughed at the idea of getting married. But this was Brooks —the one person in her life who was there for her no matter what, who loved and supported her without demanding anything in return. How could she say no? But on the other hand, how could she possibly say yes?

"Hi," Melissa said, sitting up on her bed and swinging her feet around to the floor.

Brooks came in and shut the door behind him. "I haven't seen you in a while," he said, dragging her desk chair over to the bed. He sat on it backwards, his legs straddling the sides, facing her.

Melissa nodded mutely. It had been more than a while. It had been almost a week. In fact, she hadn't spoken to him, except in passing, since the day he'd proposed.

"I know I've asked you to make a big decision,"

Brooks said, "and I realize you've needed time to think about it, but I think I deserve an answer."

Melissa felt even worse. Why did he have to be so nice and patient? Why couldn't he be irritable and nudgy so she could get mad at him the way she wanted to? She did anyway.

"You have some nerve, Brooks Baldwin," Melissa barked at him. "First you totally ruin my life, and then you actually expect me to tell you what you want to hear? Well, I have nothing to say to you right now!"

"How can you say I've ruined everything?" Brooks asked, hurt. "I'm just trying to make us both even happier than we are already."

"How will getting married make us happier?" Melissa demanded. "Did you even stop to think about the consequences of getting married so young? We're both still freshmen in college! We've each got years of school ahead of us before we should even *think* of settling down. I want to go to med school and you want to go to architecture school. What if we get into schools in different parts of the country? Is one of us supposed to give up our dream so the other one can go to the school of their choice?"

"We can work it out . . ." Brooks began.

"And what about money?" Melissa barreled on. "Weddings cost money, not to mention setting up a household. Where's that money supposed to come from if we're both students? I certainly don't have time to get a job on top of everything else I'm doing, and I don't think you do either. We're just *kids,* Brooks."

"No, Melissa, we're not," Brooks said, leaning over the top of his chair to take her hands in his. His hands felt warm and steady against her chilly, shaking ones. "Yes, we're students, but legally we're adults, and I know my feelings for you aren't the feelings of a child. I'm ready to grow up and take on adult responsibilities. And there's no reason why college—even grad school—and love can't go together. Lots of people get married at our age."

"Including my parents," Melissa said bitterly, "and look how they turned out." She pulled her hands out of Brooks's and got up to pace the room. "My parents got married right out of high school, which is not much younger than you and I are now, and they have a lousy marriage. If my mother didn't feel so sorry for my father being a helpless alcoholic, she would have divorced him long before now. Or maybe she just feels stuck. Maybe if she'd waited until she was older, she never would have married him."

"That has nothing to do with you or me," Brooks said, turning around in his chair to watch as Melissa strode between the two narrow beds like a caged tiger. "I don't have a drinking problem—I don't even drink! And we're both ambitious. We both want to make something of our lives. I'm saying that together we can do even more. We can help each other achieve what we want to achieve. We can love each other. What good is a successful career without that?"

Melissa paused in her pacing and took a deep breath. "I can't argue with that," she said, giving Brooks a pained look. "I don't want to live without love either. But why do we have to make such a big decision right now?"

"Because I don't want another relationship like the one I had with Faith, where we limp along for years, then fall apart. I either want a deep, lasting commitment, or nothing at all."

"Well, what about what I want?" Melissa shouted. "Did you ever think of that?" She shook her head. "I still can't give you an answer."

"I can't wait forever," Brooks said, getting up from the chair. "But if you need a little more time to think, you've got it. I'll get out of your way now, but I'll see you Saturday at the rafting trip. I hope you'll have an answer for me then." Brooks drew Melissa close and gave her a long hug. Then he pressed his lips against her forehead. "Just don't forget I love you," he whispered, and was gone.

* * *

At the same moment Brooks was leaving Forest Hall, KC and Peter stepped out the door of Langston House, KC's all-female study dorm. The sky was overcast and the air felt heavy and thick as they trudged across the dorm green. The distant, jagged mountains looked dismal and gray; not a good omen for KC's first professional modeling job.

"I'm going to mess up, I know it," KC said nervously to Peter. "Why don't we just go straight back to my room before I make a total fool of myself?"

"You're going to be fine," Peter reassured her, slipping his arm around her waist and tucking it into the front pocket of her forest-green slacks. "Hey," he said, worried, pulling the fabric of her slacks away from her stomach. "These feel loose on you. How much weight have you lost?"

KC leaned her head on Peter's shoulder. "Please don't start that again," she begged. "I've already explained it to you. This is a bathing suit shoot. That means almost every inch of me will be exposed."

"The few inches that are left," Peter sighed, letting his hand rest on KC's hipbone. "I know you think you look better this way, but take it from someone who's favorite hobby is looking at you. You look pale and drawn and too thin."

"The camera adds ten pounds, Peter. You should

know that," KC said. "Now do me a favor, and let's not talk about it anymore."

KC felt terrible for acting impatient with Peter when he was being so caring, but she couldn't help herself. She'd been grouchy and irritable all week, mainly because Peter was absolutely right—she hadn't been eating enough and had been feeling dizzy and weak ever since she started to diet.

KC knew she'd been pushing herself too hard. She wanted to stop; she wanted to sleep. She wanted Peter to gather her in his arms like a little kid and tuck her in and tell her everything was going to be okay. But she still wouldn't let herself admit that she needed his help.

"You know, Peter," KC said as they reached the cobbled bricks of McLaren Plaza, "it's really nice of you to walk me to the shoot, but I think I'd prefer to go the rest of the way on my own. I don't want to look—you know—unprofessional by bringing friends. They'll think I'm some giddy college kid who's never done this before."

"You are a giddy college kid who's never done this before," Peter jibed, stopping beneath a cherry tree. A chill wind brushed through the leaves over their heads.

"You know what I mean," KC said. "It's not that I don't want you to come with me . . ."

"I understand," Peter said. "I was just concerned

about getting you to the shoot in one piece. The way you look, I was afraid you might keel over before you got there."

KC straightened up and put on a bright smile. "I'm absolutely fine," she said. "Now go. I promise I'll call and tell you how it went as soon as I get back to my room."

"Don't forget to find out for me what lenses the photographer uses," Peter said.

"Will do," KC said, kissing him on the lips. Gathering all her strength, she strode across the uneven brick plaza toward the lawn surrounding the gymnasium. Though she knew Peter was looking after her with concern, she wouldn't let herself turn around. She had to act strong if she wanted to convince him—and herself—that she really was.

Once inside the gym, KC headed downstairs to the pool. The glass walls surrounding the pool were so steamy, KC could barely see in. A cardboard sign hung by the entrance, saying Pool Closed Today. Authorized Personnel Only. Too tired to feel privileged that she could enter when others would be turned away, KC pushed open the door.

Her nose was immediately assaulted by the overpowering smell of chlorine, and her eyes started to burn from the foggy air. Trying not to choke or gag, KC waved the air in front of her face so she could see better. The Olympic-size pool, a giant rectangle of aqua blue, dominated the cavernous, underground room. The water was still and clear, revealing black, parallel stripes along the bottom.

Along one side of the pool, rows of wooden bleachers climbed nearly to the ceiling. Bright photographer's lights shaded with white screens were set up at the far end of the pool by the diving board. Young men and women in rumpled jeans, T-shirts, and baseball caps, ran around moving equipment, adjusting lights, or carrying garment bags.

A long table was set up in front of the bleachers, loaded with bagels, cold cuts, fruit, soda, and candy. KC stopped and stared at the food. Maybe she could grab a bag of M&Ms, just to give her a little energy. It certainly wouldn't matter now what she ate, since the food wasn't going to have time to convert to fat and show up in the pictures.

"KC?" asked a beautiful young woman with a round face, button nose, and full lips. Her long, black hair was pulled back with a wide, purple headband which clashed fashionably with her orange and hot pink minidress.

KC extended her hand. "KC Angeletti," she said in a professional voice.

"Sunny Sun," the young woman said, shaking KC's hand energetically. Noting KC's surprised expression, she explained. "My real name's XiaoXia, but nobody can pronounce it, so everybody calls me Sunny. I'm the art director from *Western* magazine. We were really impressed with your portfolio. You've got wonderful bones."

KC ran nervous fingers over her hips. Sunny was going to see a lot of bone today. Suddenly KC worried that she had lost too much weight, but Sunny was smiling and gesturing KC to follow her to the far end of the pool where the lights were set up.

"We've got three models scheduled for today," Sunny explained cheerfully, "and we're going to do group shots as well as individual shots. Kathy!" Sunny called to a thin, blond woman with several garment bags slung over her shoulder. Kathy approached them. "This is Kathy Holohan. She'll be in charge of wardrobe. And since the lights are just about set up, Kathy, why don't you give KC her first change and we'll get started. The other two models are here already, so we'll try a three-shot by the diving board."

"We've got a tent set up over here," Kathy explained, leading KC to a make-shift changing area made of free-standing nylon partitions. "We're women!" she announced as she pushed one of the partitions aside so she and KC could enter.

Two of the most gorgeous women KC had ever seen in her life were being zipped into skintight tank suits. One had long, platinum-blond hair that reached nearly to her waist and enormous blue eyes. The other, a tall, black woman, had a full head of soft, fuzzy hair, a heart-shaped face, and a drop-dead figure. KC couldn't believe that she'd actually been chosen to model with them. They were perfect-looking. She even thought she recognized one of them from *Vogue* magazine. How could she compete with top models? She was just a college student doing this for extra money.

"Here's your suit," Kathy said, handing KC a shiny, black, Lycra two-piece suit. It was more fully cut than a bikini, but it had high-cut legs and a plunging neckline.

KC was still finding it difficult to breathe in the acrid air. "Is it just me," she asked the others, "or did they put too much chlorine in the pool?"

"Oh, that's the photographer's chemical fog machine," Kathy explained, hanging the garment bags on a metal stand set up inside the tent. "I know it smells bitter, but it softens the lights to give the shots a more romantic look."

KC nodded, trying not to show how much she was bothered by it. "I'll be ready in just a minute," she said, slipping out of her slacks.

After KC was dressed, Kathy gave her a white cotton cover-up to throw over her suit. "This way, ladies," she said, leading KC, Daniella, and Jennifer to some folding directors' chairs. A plump man dressed in black was waiting there with his makeup kit and hairbrush.

If KC hadn't been feeling so tired and hungry, she might have been able to enjoy this star treatment. The photographer, a blond man named Gerhard, oohed and aahed over her like she was as much a cover girl as the other models. The makeup man went into ecstasy over her high cheekbones. A young intern with an eager expression asked if she wanted hot tea or coffee; if only he'd offered a hamburger or french fries.

At last, Gerhard deemed the models ready and set up his shot. He had Daniella and Jennifer sit back to back on the diving board while KC stood behind them, at the edge of the board. Gerhard told her to lean forward and place her hands on her knees. Then he backed away, checked them through his viewfinder, and pronounced them perfect.

"This will just take a few minutes," Gerhard promised as he signaled an assistant to adjust one of the lights so that it was shining directly into KC's eyes. KC didn't want to close her eyes even for a second because she was afraid she'd lose her balance and fall into the pool. Between the foggy, humid air and her empty stomach, she was starting to feel faint.

"Okay," Gerhard said as he began to click the

shutter. "Have fun with it. Let go. That's good, girls. Show me you're having a good time."

KC tried to smile as Daniella and Jennifer were doing. She tried to ignore her discomfort and focus on showing off her bones to their best advantage.

"Just a few more," Gerhard assured them ten minutes later as he pulled a finished roll out of the camera and loaded another. "I know you're getting a little tired, but this looks so good to me. Daniella, Jennifer, turn toward each other a little bit, throw your hair forward, that's right. KC, don't move a muscle. Very good."

KC's legs were starting to shake from holding the same position for so long. How many pictures could he take of this one pose? Didn't he have anything else he wanted to try? If KC didn't get off that diving board soon, they were going to have one stiff model.

"Okay, girls, that's it!" Gerhard told them finally. "Take a break."

Jennifer and Daniella scooted off the diving board. KC followed behind, balancing as if she were a tightrope walker. She grabbed her cover-up and searched for a place to lie down for just a minute. If she didn't, she wasn't going to make it through the rest of the shoot. But where could she go? She couldn't let anyone see her, or they'd know something was wrong.

It looked dark and quiet under the bleachers. She could slip under there and sit down for a second, until she got her strength back. As fast as she dared, KC padded over the concrete pavement surrounding the pool and ducked beneath the bleachers.

Placing her cover-up beneath her on the ground so she wouldn't snag the swim suit, KC sat down on the hard ground and leaned back against one of the metal supports. Why was she sweating? It wasn't as hot under here. But KC was too tired to think about it. All she wanted was to close her eyes, just for a second.

When KC awoke, she was lying flat on her back on the cool pavement. How had she gotten there? Had she passed out? And what was that smell? It wasn't chlorine. It was a much better sort of smell. KC sniffed the air, trying to determine what it was.

"What are we going to do with you?" a motherly voice asked above her head.

KC didn't recognize the voice, but she was able to make out a mass of orange curls. The person above her leaned down, and KC was aware of an abundant body stuffed into tight clothes, and lips that were bright red.

"Okay, okay, I know you're wondering what I'm doing here," Liza said, "and I guess I might as well tell you the truth. I crashed, okay? I remembered you mentioned the photo shoot when we were in the student union, and I was dying to see what was going on. Faith let slip when and where it was taking place. I thought maybe the photographer would discover me or something. I do have interesting features, you know, even if I am a little full-figured for a bathing suit like yours."

"How long have I been out?" KC asked in alarm. By now, Sunny had probably called the modeling agency and told them never to send her on another job again.

"Not more than thirty seconds," Liza said. "Don't worry. Your secret's safe with me. But you look pale as a ghost. Have you been eating lately?"

KC shook her head regretfully and pulled herself up to a sitting position. "I wanted to look good for the shoot, but I think I might have overdone it."

"Exactly what I thought," Liza said, holding out a cup of hot soup and a plastic spoon. "You'd better eat this right away," she said. "And don't worry. I took a couple of spoonfuls, but I don't have a cold or anything."

KC felt her mouth water. The delicious smell came from the soup. She allowed Liza to spoon some into her mouth. The warm, tasty liquid felt so good going down, and the vegetables were tasty and filling.

"Now take some juice," Liza said, handing KC a

paper cup. "Your blood sugar's probably down. You need sugar for energy."

KC sipped the cool, thick, orange juice and felt her tastebuds tingle at the unfamiliar sensation of flavors touching her tongue. Her head was beginning to clear already.

"More soup," Liza commanded, making KC finish the rest.

KC smiled up at Liza as she drained both cups.

"Well?" Liza asked, standing up and planting her fists against her thick hips.

"I feel a lot better," KC said. "Thanks. You saved my life."

Liza helped KC to her feet. "Glad I could be of help," she said. "If anyone asks what I'm doing here, just tell them I'm your manager."

KC smiled as she and Liza came out from behind the bleachers.

"There you are, KC," Kathy called, spotting them and waving a red maillot. "I need you to change for your next shot."

Liza winked and headed back for the food table. "Never turn down a free meal, that's my motto," she said.

KC walked back to the changing tent with renewed strength. She was still starving, but at least she'd have enough energy to finish the shoot. She'd even allow herself a bagel at the next break. And after what Liza had done for her, she wasn't the least bit worried about standing up for Liza if anyone asked what she was doing there. She was glad to have a familiar face with her.

KC thought back to how badly Peter had wanted to accompany her. Why had it seemed so important to push him away? It all seemed so silly in retrospect. She'd been so concerned with being independent, yet all she'd done was prove how much she needed people.

Having Peter around wasn't going to make her a weak, passive, needy female. Why hadn't she realized that before? And how long did she expect Peter to keep sticking around if she kept acting like she could easily live without him? He had to be a glutton for punishment to put up with her this long. It was definitely time for a change. Hard as it would be, KC was going to drop her defenses and let him know how much she really needed him.

There was someone else KC owed a lot to, someone else who'd been there for her when she needed it the most. KC also had to admit that she was grateful to her new friend, Liza Ruff.

Eleven

"Are you the pied piper, Byron?" Josh asked as the two of them walked down Chapel Street, away from campus. Behind them, a long line of Winnie's friends stretched out along the sidewalk. Winnie came first, chatting happily with Faith about the computer fair coming up later in the evening. Winnie had dressed up especially for the occasion, in silver tights with gray shorts, a boxy, gray vest, and her jingle bell boots. She called it her "robot" outfit and was telling everyone she was Alphie's sister.

Alphie, Josh's robot, was sleeping peacefully, locked in a lab at the computer center. In just a few hours, though, Josh would activate him and hopefully impress everyone who'd come to the exhibition, or at least some of the engineers and designers who'd be there from the major computer companies. Josh was hoping to get an internship this summer at one of those firms.

Behind Winnie and Faith, KC and Lauren walked arm in arm with Liza. Josh was surprised Liza had been invited since Winnie had told him no one liked her. But KC and Lauren were practically hanging onto her and acting like she was their best friend. Peter walked along next to KC, his ever-present camera hanging around his neck.

Behind KC, Lauren, and Liza, Faith's next-door neighbor Kimberly leaned dreamily against her boyfriend Derek. Kimberly was a tall, slender, black freshman with close-cut hair and a long, graceful neck. She used to be a dance major, but lately Josh had been seeing a lot of her in the science building, where she hung out with Derek, who was a science wiz. Derek was also on the fencing team and about a hundred school committees.

"Dad!" Winnie came bounding forward and danced around Byron and Josh as they walked. "It was so nice of you to invite all my friends for pizza. I know it's a lot of people," she apologized.

Byron grinned and his whole face lit up. "I'm just happy my daughter has so many friends," he said. "Takes after her old man."

Winnie led her father around the corner, and they came upon Luigi's Restaurant, a white, stucco building festooned with red, white, and green streamers. Winnie opened the door, and Josh's nostrils were filled with the aroma of warm marinara sauce and baking dough. Inside, the restaurant was decorated with garish frescoes of the Italian countryside and boot-shaped maps of Italy. In one corner, a little old man with an accordion played Italian folk songs.

"Isn't this great?" Winnie asked her father. "It's so tacky, that's why I love it."

"And they make a super pizza," Josh added as everyone crowded in the entrance.

"My mouth is watering already," Byron said as the hostess led them to the corner of the dining room where several tables had been pushed together. The table was set with plastic dishes, flimsy, aluminum silverware, and paper napkin dispensers. Everyone scrambled for chairs. Josh ended up between Winnie and KC, and Byron planted himself at the head of the table.

A plump waitress appeared with menus and baskets of garlic bread. Her nametag read "Elda." Byron leaped to his feet and kissed her hand. "Beautiful Elda!" he said. "You don't know how happy we are to see you. We're starving!" Elda looked tickled as she took her hand back and opened up her notepad. "Pizza for everybody!" Byron proclaimed with a sweeping gesture of his hand. "We want mushrooms, we want pepperoni, we want anchovies, we want everything you've got!"

"Ewww!" Winnie giggled. "Not anchovies!"

"Okay," Byron said, putting his arm around Elda, who didn't seem to mind one bit. "Lose the anchovies. Bring us, oh, four large pizzas for the table, two with everything but anchovies, and two plain. Then how about a couple of huge bowls of spaghetti with meat sauce, and a couple of big Caesar salads."

"Yay!" Winnie applauded, while everyone else whistled, hooted, and gave the thumbs-up sign.

"And since I'm sure that won't be enough . . ." Byron continued.

"Daaaad," Winnie complained. "We'll burst!"

"Worry about that tomorrow," Byron said. "I was just going to say we'd need something to wash it down with. Let's say some pitchers of soda and beer. Make that diet soda for the ladies."

"Right," Peter said. "We don't want the girls to ruin their diets."

"*What* diet?" KC said, as she threw a balled up paper napkin at Peter from across the table. She started chomping on her second piece of garlic bread. "I never want to hear that word again as long as I live. Unless I turn into a fat pig, in which case, Peter, I want you to wire my lips together."

"You have a long way to go before you get to that point," said Liza, who sat next to KC. "Me, on the other hand . . ." She started to reach for the bread basket, then stopped herself.

"Oh, go ahead," KC said. "Live. Enjoy. You know my motto—never turn down a free meal."

KC and Liza started laughing hysterically.

"That's the spirit," Byron said. As Elda returned carrying pitchers and stacks of plastic glasses, Byron raced to take them from her. "I'll do the honors," he told her. He set glasses in front of everyone and poured beverages. "Now," he said, returning to his seat and holding up a glass of beer. "I'd like to propose a toast. We have a lot of things to celebrate tonight, so feel free to chime in if I've left anything out. First of all, I'd like to thank all of you for joining my daughter and me tonight. I hope I'll get a chance to know each of you better. I'd also like to toast Josh, who's done so much to bring Winnie and me back together, and who's about to take the world by storm tonight at the computer fair.

"Most of all, I'd like to toast my daughter Winnie, who's grown into a lovely, lively, young woman filled with charm and effervescence. My only regret is that I wasn't there to watch her grow up, but I'm glad I'll be a part of her life from here on in."

"Here, here!" Faith shouted. Everyone clicked their plastic glasses together.

Winnie stood up on her chair and clapped her hands. "Excuse me!" she shouted giddily, shaking one of her jingle bell boots. "My dad *did* leave something out. Something very important." Winnie's eyes shone with happy tears. "I'd like to toast Byron Jennings. In just the short time we've been back together, he's made me feel very lucky to have such a special, caring, and generous father. I'm sorry for all the years we've missed, but it's never too late to start."

"Right!" Josh and the others cheered, raising their glasses as Winnie did a little jig on her chair.

Winnie sat back down and kissed Josh on the cheek. "I can't thank you enough for what you did," she whispered. "You're so good for me."

One hour, four pizzas, and several tons of pasta later, everyone was groaning and clutching their stomachs.

"It's a good thing I'm not going on the rafting trip tomorrow," Peter said. "I'd probably sink the boat."

"This was delicious," Winnie said, hugging her father. "Thanks a lot for treating us."

Josh pushed himself away from the table. "I need some fresh air," he said. "I'll be right back."

Josh lumbered toward the front door of Luigi's and made his way outside. A cool, spring breeze wafted down from the mountains, bringing the scent of pine with it. Josh was pretty pleased with himself. He knew how hard it had been for Winnie to open up to her father, but it had all turned out well. Byron hadn't been an ogre after all. He was just misunderstood. And Winnie was much happier now that she'd taken the risk of getting to know him. Josh was glad he'd pushed Winnie this time.

Feeling refreshed, Josh went back inside the restaurant and saw Byron standing by the cash register, still flirting with Elda. Byron handed her a credit card to pay the bill and waited, whistling, while she ran it through the machine.

Elda looked down at the electronic display on the credit card machine and frowned. "I'm sorry," she said. "For some reason, I can't get an approval on your credit card."

Byron seemed unconcerned. "Try it again," he said. "There must be some mistake."

"I'm sure that's it, Byron," Elda said, sliding the plastic card through the magnetic slot again. Josh had to chuckle. *What a charmer Byron was,* he thought. Already he and the waitress were on a first name basis.

This time, though, Elda looked truly upset. "I don't understand it!" she said. "Maybe there's something wrong with our machine." She ran the card through a third time. "Do you have any other cards I could try?" she asked.

Byron searched through his wallet. "Just my luck," he said. "I left my other cards in the safe at the hotel, and I only have about twenty dollars cash. This is so embarrassing. I don't know what to say."

Josh could just imagine Winnie's face when Byron came back to the table and told her that he couldn't afford to pay for dinner. She'd be so embarrassed in front of all her friends. And she'd feel like her father had let her down again, even if it was just an oversight on Byron's part. Josh couldn't let Winnie's happy night be ruined.

Josh appeared at Byron's side. "I couldn't help overhearing," he said.

"This is totally embarrassing," Byron said. "I'm contesting a charge on this card, so they've probably put a temporary hold on it. I can't believe I didn't bring any of my other cards. I have six back at the hotel."

"It's okay. Maybe I can help. I don't have much cash either, but I could write a check. My bank's here in town," Josh said to Elda.

Elda nodded sympathetically. "I'll just need to see some ID," she said, passing him the bill.

When Josh saw the total, he nearly passed out. Dinner for ten cost over $150! That was about half of Josh's entire checking account and he needed cash for the next day's raft trip. But he had no choice. He couldn't let Winnie down. Josh swallowed hard and wrote out the check.

"You're a lifesaver," Byron said. "And I promise you, I'll pay you back in full tomorrow. I've got some traveler's checks at the hotel, which you can cash anywhere."

"No problem," Josh said. "By the way, you don't have to tell Winnie what happened. It can be our secret."

Byron winked. "I knew I liked you from the very beginning."

With many thanks to Byron, everyone got up from the table and strolled back to campus. Winnie was so joyful, so excited, that Josh quickly forgot the incident at the cash register. He was sure Byron would pay him back. Anyway, he had a lot more important things to think about—the computer fair was about to begin.

"This is amazing!" Winnie said, as their crowd entered the softly lit lobby. The computer center was a brand new building made entirely of burnished steel. The blue-gray walls shone dully, and the floor was covered with a pale, gray industrial carpet. At different points along the walls, colorful monitors blinked cheerfully, providing information menus and computer-generated graphic art. There was no permanent furniture of any kind, but the walls curved outward near the floor, becoming low banks of seating, covered with pale, gray cushions.

"I feel like I'm *inside* a computer," Kimberly declared.

"You are, in a way," Josh informed her. "A computer helped design this place." He led them to the enormous conference room where the fair was being held. The room was filled with rows of booths. Some were slick, colorful displays featuring state-of-the-art computers from IBM, Apple, and other large manufacturers. Others, like Josh's, were more makeshift, using older computers to demonstrate new software programs.

The aisles between the booths were already filled with dozens of people, looking in awe at the futuristic technology. No one had a robot like Alphie, though. Josh was hoping that Alphie would be the hit of the show.

"I'll see you guys in a minute," Josh said, ducking down the hall to the lab where he'd hidden Alphie. He wanted Alphie to make a big entrance.

"I'll come with you," Byron said. "I've been dying to see your invention. Winnie wouldn't tell me a word about it. She says you swore her to secrecy."

Josh nodded as he and Byron left the others. "I'll let Alphie speak for himself," he said. "You'll see." Josh pulled a ring of keys out of the pocket of his jeans and opened a laboratory door. The room was dark, but Josh didn't turn on the light. He just pulled a small, remote control device out of his other pocket and pressed a button.

"You rrrang?" asked a high, nasal voice. Colorful Christmas lights started flashing on and off, and Alphie emerged from the dark. His black sphere of a head pivoted from side to side, and his infrared light winked deep inside.

"Amazing!" Byron exclaimed.

"You haven't seen anything yet," Josh said as Alphie rolled past them and headed down the hall to the conference room.

"How does he know where to go?" Byron asked.

"He sees the same as you or me," Josh explained. "Only his eye is an infrared sensor. He can turn corners, though, and he knows how to get to every room in this building. I've programmed directions into his software."

"You're a genius!" said Byron, impressed. "I've got to see more."

Josh and Byron reached the doorway of the conference room just in time to hear Alphie address an older couple near the door. "Can you show me the way to booth 18?" he asked.

The man and woman roared with laughter, and people started crowding around Alphie to see what he'd do next.

"Pardon me. *Scusi. Excusez-moi,*" Alphie said cheerfully as he wheeled his way to Josh's booth. The sign Josh had printed out on the lab's laser printer announced ALPHIE—MAN'S NEW BEST FRIEND. Josh and Byron followed Alphie to the booth.

"This is a marketer's dream!" Byron said. "There are so many applications for something like this. You could program it to get sodas from the refrigerator for people who are too lazy to get up during TV commercials."

"I thought of that," Josh said. "Actually . . ."

"You could mold one shaped like a dog," Byron went on excitedly. "Then you could really call it man's best friend. It could get your slippers or retrieve bones. You could even put in a voice chip so it could bark like a dog."

"I know," Josh said. "In fact . . ."

"This robot is very impressive," said the man who'd been standing by the door when Alphie had walked out. He wore a suit and tie and had a full head of white hair. "Can you tell me more about it?"

"Byron Jennings," Byron said, shaking the man's hand before Josh had a chance to step forward.

"Malcolm Winters," the older man said. "National Equipment Corporation; executive vice president of research and development."

"I can see you've already spotted a winner," Byron said, kneeling beside Alphie. "He's a cute little fella, isn't he? But there's more to Alphie than meets the eye. Much more. It's the programming that makes Alphie special. And there are dozens of commercial applications. My company's already doing quantitative research in several test markets, so if you're interested, you'll have to wait in line."

Josh looked at Byron in surprise. What was he talking about? Byron had never even seen Alphie until a few minutes ago. And why was he doing all the talking when it was Josh's invention?

"Byron . . ." Josh tried to cut in.

Byron winked and whispered, "Trust me. The best way to drum up interest is to act like it's already a hot item."

"What a cute little robot!" a young woman said. "I'm a toy manufacturer, and a smaller version of this might be perfect for our fall line."

"Why thank you," Byron said, adjusting his tie and treating her to the same smile he'd used on the waitress at the restaurant. "My colleague here, and I spent a lot of time working on it just so we could impress someone like you."

The woman smiled coyly at Byron as the two leaned down to get a closer look at the robot. Josh was beginning to get a funny feeling in his stomach. First, there was the credit card problem. Now Byron was taking over Josh's exhibit, sweet-talking everyone in sight, and even lying about his involvement with Alphie. Josh began to wonder if he'd been a little hasty in encouraging Winnie to open up to her father.

For the next three hours, Josh could barely get near his robot. By the time the fair was over, Josh was ready to explode. He hadn't talked to any of the representatives from the computer companies. It wouldn't have mattered anyway. Everyone who was there probably thought Byron was the inventor, not Josh.

Josh stood at a distance, while Byron kissed Winnie good-bye, and left the fair with the young woman from the toy company. *What a charmer,* Josh thought for the second time that night, only this time it didn't seem funny at all. As Winnie approached him, all aglow, Josh wrestled with himself. Should he say anything to her or not? He didn't want to destroy her happiness, but if there was something odd about her father, didn't Josh have a duty to tell her?

"Hi, you two!" Winnie said, kissing first Josh, then Alphie. "I just don't know which one of you is cuter."

Josh gave Winnie a curt hug. "Come on," he said. "Let's put Alphie to bed, then I'll walk you over to Swedenborg House."

"Thanks," Winnie said, bounding down the hall beside him in her jingle bell boots. "I know it's sort of late to start decorating for the benefit tomorrow night, but this is the only time anybody could do it. We all lead such busy lives."

Josh nodded silently.

"What's the matter?" Winnie asked. "You seem kind of quiet."

Josh let Alphie back into the lab and locked the door. "It's nothing," he said. "I'm just tired, I guess."

"KC and Peter already left for Swedenborg House half an hour ago," Winnie chattered as they left the computer center, "so some of the decorations will already be up when we get there. It's really nice of you to help me out after the long day you've had. I bet you just want to go back to your room and get some sleep."

Josh nodded, although the last thing he thought he could do tonight was sleep. Especially if he didn't tell Winnie that maybe her mother had been right all along—maybe her father *was* undependable. Maybe Winnie would have been better off if he'd just let her make her own decisions instead of butting in.

"Here we are!" Winnie exclaimed as they neared Swedenborg House. The oldest structure on campus, it was a small, white, shingled building with one large room inside. Bright chandeliers hung overhead, filling the room with a light that was visible from all over campus. The outside of the building was adorned with "cookie cutter" cornices so that it looked like a gingerbread house.

The front door was open, and Josh could see KC and Peter setting up folding chairs in neat rows in front of a freestanding wooden platform. Courtney Conner, the president of KC's sorority, Tri Beta, was hanging construction paper cut-outs of red telephones and laughing faces on the plain, white walls. Her blond hair fluffed about her shoulders and she wore a sweater dress and pearls; she looked like she should be going to a dinner party.

"Hi, you guys," Winnie said. "You're so nice for helping me. David and Teresa promised they'll be here bright and early tomorrow morning to do the rest."

"We're happy to help," Courtney said in her honey-smooth voice. "Some of the Tri Beta sisters will be by tomorrow also."

"Wait 'til you get a load of our sign," Winnie said

to Josh, dragging him to a large piece of plywood leaning against one wall. "I got Dmitri, an art major in Faith's dorm, to paint it for us." Grabbing one end of the sign, she pulled it away from the wall so Josh could see it. The huge sign had a bright, yellow background. A large, accurate caricature of Karl Fanfield's head perched on a tiny body, and bright, red letters announced Karl Fanfield Live! In the lower right corner was the same logo of a red phone and the caption, The Hotline's Hot!

"I can't wait 'til tomorrow night," Winnie said, leaning the sign back against the wall. "I still can't believe Karl Fanfield's coming here, to Springfield. He must be such a nice man to do this as a favor to my father. Although, on the other hand, my father's so nice it's no wonder people love him. Don't you think my father's the nicest man you ever met? Not that you don't love your own father, of course, but wouldn't you say my dad's definitely in the top two? Yours being the other one, of course."

Here was his opening. If Josh was going to say anything to Winnie about Byron, he'd better say it now. If he didn't, it might be too late, and he'd never forgive himself. "Uh, actually, Winnie," Josh began, "I sort of wanted to talk to you about that. I'm beginning to wonder how great a guy he really is."

"What do you mean?" Winnie asked, grabbing a

pair of folding chairs and setting them up at the end of a long row.

Josh followed her with two more chairs. "Please don't be mad at me for saying this, but I think I've seen another side to your father that maybe I should tell you about."

"What other side?" Winnie asked, her small face pale.

Josh explained about Byron's credit card and his behavior at the computer fair. "I'm not telling you this to upset you," he said. "I just want you to be aware of it in case he turns out to be a flake after all. I don't want you to be too disappointed."

Winnie's brown eyes grew hard, and a deep furrow appeared between her eyebrows. "I can't believe you!" she shouted. "Are you schizophrenic or something? You're the one who bulldozed me into trusting him in the first place! Make up your mind! Or are you trying to drive me crazy?"

"Of course I'm not," Josh said, trying to stay calm. "I'm just saying new evidence has come to light."

"You talk like a lawyer. And you're not making sense. You're going to let those two, tiny things tonight change your whole perception of him? Everybody's got faults, you know. Even you."

"We're not talking about me," Josh said, trying to ignore the insult. "I'm not saying I've changed my whole perception of your father. He could still be terrific. I'm just saying we should be openminded to his bad qualities as well as good."

Winnie crossed her arms and nodded knowingly. "I just figured it out," she said. "This isn't *really* about my father, is it? You're just jealous! You're jealous that my father stole your thunder at your stupid exhibition tonight. You're jealous that he has a way of talking to people that makes them feel special. No wonder everybody wanted to talk to him instead of you."

"My stupid exhibition?" Josh thundered. "Oh, that's real supportive. Exactly what a loving girl-friend's supposed to say. For your information, my exhibition isn't any stupider than your stupid bene-fit! I don't know why I even came over here to help you in the first place." Josh was aware that KC, Peter, and Courtney had stopped working long ago and were listening quietly to this argument, but he was too angry to stop himself.

"Oh!" Winnie cried, stamping her foot on the wooden floor. "So now my father's a sleaze and my benefit's stupid? Well, if you think it's so stupid, you can just skip it. Believe me, you won't be missed!"

"Fine!" Josh shouted. "I've got better things to do with my time, anyway!" Letting the metal fold-ing chair in his hand drop to the floor with a crash, Josh charged past KC, Peter, and Courtney. After all they'd been through, after all the work they'd done to get their relationship back on track, it was over again. The last thing Josh heard as he stormed out of Swedenborg House was the sound of Winnie bursting into tears.

Twelve

·····································

Aaaannnghhhhhhhhh!

The downstairs buzzer jolted Lauren awake Saturday morning with its loud, insistent whine. She sat up in bed and rubbed the sleep from her eyes. Her studio apartment was small and cramped, but at least it was finally comfortable. Lauren had saved up to buy a used futon sleep-sofa, and her friends had donated most of the other furnishings. Winnie had contributed the fishnetting that hung on the wall above the futon, Faith had given her large theatrical posters, which Lauren had had framed, and KC had helped her build shelves to hold her TV and computer. Kimberly had contributed half a dozen healthy plants which sat beneath

the two narrow windows on tables donated by
Courtney from the Tri Beta basement.

Aaaaannnngghhhhhh!

"Okay, okay," Lauren told the buzzer, hopping
out of bed and plodding across the floor in her bare
feet. She was still so full from last night's Italian
foodfest, that it was hard to move quickly. It probably wasn't a real visitor, anyway. No one ever came
this far off campus. The only people who rang her
bell were drunks who wanted to sleep in the vesti-
bule at night.

"Yes?" Lauren asked, pressing the talk button.

"Lauren, it's Dash!" came a voice over the anti-
quated speaker.

"Dash!" Lauren cried joyfully, pressing the button so Dash could enter. It had been almost two
weeks since she'd seen his face. The last time she'd
spoken to him through the door of his apartment,
he'd said he was feeling a little better, but she
hadn't expected him to get out of bed so soon.

Lauren raced to the bathroom to wash her face
and brush her teeth. She threw a white terrycloth
robe over her flannel nightgown before her door-
bell rang. After peering through the peephole, just
to be sure it was really Dash, Lauren unbolted the
locks and unchained the chain.

"Dash!" she cried joyfully, throwing herself into
his arms. His lean, muscular body felt thinner than

normal, but it felt so good to press her face against the soft cotton of his olive-green army jacket and to smell his clean scent of lemons and soap. Suddenly she remembered his measles and stepped back abruptly. "Are you contagious?"

Dash laughed. "Do you think I would come near you if I were contagious? Of course not." He grabbed Lauren's hand and pulled her into her apartment. "The health center just pronounced me cured, and I wanted you to be the first to know."

"Hooray!" Lauren cried, clapping her hands. "I guess that means it's okay to kiss you, right?"

Dash gazed down at Lauren. His dark hair was scruffy and his face was covered with a few days' growth of stubble, but to Lauren, he'd never looked better. "You'd better kiss me," he whispered softly. "Looking forward to kissing you has been the only thing that kept me going the past two weeks."

Lauren felt a thrill of pleasure as Dash pulled her toward him and planted his hungry lips on hers. Her lips were hungry too. It was the most exciting wake-up kiss she'd ever had. At last they broke apart and Lauren took the few steps into her tiny kitchen. "Would you like some breakfast?" she asked. "I bet aside from the food I left outside your door, all you ate while you were sick was pizza. When you ate at all that is."

"You've got that right," said Dash, who ate pizza nearly every night, even when he was well. "But actually, I can't stay. I passed our editor, Greg Sukamaki, on my way across campus this morning. He asked me to stop by the *Journal* office at eleven o'clock to give me an important new assignment."

"What a slavedriver," Lauren laughed. "You've been out of bed for an hour, and he's already got his hooks into you. Oh, well. I guess that's because you're such a talented writer."

"I do want to see you, though," Dash said. "What are you doing tonight?"

"I'm working, remember?" For the past few months, Lauren had been working as a maid at the Springfield Inn.

"Right," Dash said. "Say, why don't you stop by my place afterward. I'm going to prove you wrong."

"Huh?" Lauren looked up at him questioningly.

"Pizza's not the *only* thing I ever eat," Dash said. "In fact, though you may not know it, I'm an excellent cook. So come over after work, and I'll prepare my famous Chicken Marbella, by candlelight of course."

"Sounds incredibly romantic," Lauren said brushing her lips over Dash's neck. "I can hardly wait!"

* * *

"We're going to be encountering some pretty rough water," said Susan Gluck, the whitewater rafting guide for Melissa's boat. "I'm not saying this to scare you, but simply to prepare you."

Melissa sat on the edge of a heavy-duty inflatable raft which was perched on the rocky shore of the Wahalla River. Brooks sat in front of her on the same side of the boat. Josh sat across from her in the back, and Phoenix Cates sat in front of Josh. Phoenix, a long-haired freshman from Rapids Hall was Courtney's ex-boyfriend. All four wore shorts and T-shirts under orange lifevests. On their heads, were white, bicycle-style helmets strapped under their chins.

Susan, a petite, muscular woman, stood on the rocks outside the boat, her hand propped up on a wooden paddle. Half a dozen other boats were scattered on the rocks all around them, filled with other Springfield students. The churning waters of the Wahalla hurled themselves against the rocks, lapping eagerly at the rafts as if they couldn't wait to swallow them up.

Why did I let Brooks talk me into this? Melissa thought as she tried to focus on the safety instructions Susan was giving them. *As if I didn't have enough to worry about, now I have to focus on keeping my feet inside the toe-holds so I don't fall out of the boat.* Even if Melissa did get back to shore alive, she'd have a much bigger problem to tackle when she got out of the boat—Brooks's marriage proposal. Brooks hadn't said anything about it again, but Melissa knew he was expecting an answer today.

"Even if you do fall out of the boat," Susan was saying, "*don't panic*. Just remember to relax and keep your feet in front of you as you're carried down the rapids. I won't jump in after you since I have to stay in the boat with the other passengers. But we'll meet you at the end of the run and throw you this float." Susan lifted up what looked like an inflated bag attached to a long rope. "When the float reaches you, hang on to it while we reel you in, then keep your body limp as we pull you into the boat. Don't try to help us or climb in on your own; you'll just upset the boat. Any questions?"

Josh raised his hand. "I know you say it's not dangerous if we fall in, but that water looks pretty choppy. And aren't there rocks and things? Couldn't we hit our heads?"

"Not if you keep your feet in front of you at all times," Susan said. "The worst thing that will happen is your feet will hit the rocks first and you'll get a couple of bruises. I should also mention that you'll encounter suck holes. These are whirlpools of water that will suck you under the surface for a few seconds, but don't worry—they'll toss you up again. Just hold your breath and relax."

"Relax?" Josh whispered across the boat to Melissa. "After this 'safety' talk, I feel less safe than before she opened her mouth. I don't even know why I bothered to come today. I've got a terrible headache." Melissa had heard from Winnie about her fight with Josh after the computer fair. Winnie had cried on and off all night. It seemed Josh wasn't any happier than she was that they'd broken up again.

"Okay," Susan said. "We're ready to go. Please step out of the boat and drag it into the stream over here. Then, when you're up to your knees in water, climb in and we'll start paddling."

Melissa stepped out of the boat and helped pull it into the stream. She tried not to shriek as her sneakers hit the freezing water. The rocks were slippery under her feet, and it took every bit of control she had not to fall in. After they'd moved forward a few yards, everyone clambered in, sat down, and hooked their feet in the toe-holds. Grabbing her paddle, Melissa braced herself as the boat was carried along by the ever-increasing current.

"Start paddling," Susan directed them, steering them away from the other boats which were also starting out.

Melissa dipped her paddle in the water and tried to stroke evenly with the others. Though they were moving fast, the ride was smooth. Above the craggy riverbanks were gently sloping hillsides with groves of juniper trees alternating with grassy meadows. Overhead, a flock of wild geese flew in formation. Melissa looked toward the other riverbank and saw a fawn-colored deer eating leaves off a juniper tree. The air smelled clean and fresh, but Melissa was too miserable to enjoy it all.

Ahead of her, Brooks barely looked to either side. Melissa knew he wasn't thinking about wildlife either. He was wondering what she was going to tell him. Melissa didn't know herself, but she had to make up her mind. It wasn't fair to keep him hanging any longer.

"The Wahalla River is protected by the 'Wild and Scenic Protection Act,'" Susan narrated as they paddled, "which means generations to come will be able to ride these pristine rapids as you're doing now. The surrounding lands have also been preserved, including the ancient Wahalla Indian burial grounds and the Oak Ridge frontier settlement, which we'll be passing on your left in just a few seconds."

Melissa saw the remains of an old Western town. There were still signs on some of the old wooden buildings. One was a general store with a hitching post out front. Another, with swinging wooden doors, was McGregor's Saloon.

"This is great!" Phoenix exclaimed. "It's like a Western movie come to life!"

"If we're lucky," Susan continued, "we might see a bald eagle. But right now, it's time to hang on to your hats. We're about to hit our first rapid, Devil's Canyon."

"Oh great," Josh said as the ride started getting bumpy and the boat began to spin. "As if my headache weren't bad enough, now we're heading into a giant Mixmaster."

"Just hang on," Susan warned them. "There are a lot of rocks in this part of the run. I'll steer you around them, but we're going to get tossed a bit."

At that moment, the raft was swept up on a rising wave, then dropped straight down with a rough jerk.

"Ungh!" Josh groaned. "I think I'm getting seasick."

"This is super!" Phoenix shouted over the roar of the water. "It's just like riding a bucking bronco!"

Brooks looked relaxed, but said nothing. He just paddled listlessly.

"Here comes the good part!" Susan shouted as the boat was swept up again, then flew off the top of the wave and dove down. The rocking motion was repeated over and over. It really was like riding a wild, uncontrollable horse at breakneck speed.

Melissa felt cold water slap her in the face every time the boat crashed down.

"I don't feel so good," Josh said as the boat rose to the crest of the highest wave yet.

Brooks turned around at Josh's words. "Don't worry," he said. "You'll get used—"

"Look out!" Susan shouted. The boat dropped with dizzying speed, and Melissa heard a sickening thud as they hit something solid. The force of the impact sent them all reeling. Melissa was able to grip the toe-holds with her feet, but Brooks went flying over the side of the boat. Melissa pawed at her eyes, nearly blinded by the water, as she tried to see where Brooks had gone. For a moment, she could see the white of his helmet, but then he disappeared under the seething, roiling foam.

"Oh no!" Melissa screamed. "He'll drown!"

"Stay calm!" Susan told her. "He'll come up any second. You'll see."

Melissa waited, searching the churning water that held her boyfriend in its clutches. Jagged rocks reared up every few yards like shark's teeth, waiting to dig in. It seemed like hours had gone by, but there was still no sign of him. Though the boat still rocked dangerously, Melissa stood up so she could see better.

"Sit down!" Susan screamed. "We'll find him! Don't worry!"

Melissa didn't listen. She couldn't stay on the boat when there was the slightest chance of saving Brooks. So heedless of the rules, she flung down her paddle and jumped into the icy river.

Thirteen

••••••••••••••••••••••••••

"I've got the T-shirts!" Winnie announced Saturday afternoon as she backed through the door of Swedenborg House. "This carton holds six dozen T-shirts. I hope it's enough."

"Let me help you with that," Faith said, rushing down the central aisle between the folding chairs. Her long blond hair was loose, and she wore a denim jumper and T-shirt. She grabbed one end of the box and the two of them carried it to a long table set up along a side wall.

Lauren, dressed in a black pullover sweater and olive drab army pants, had just finished covering the table with a red paper tablecloth. Now she was hand-lettering an oaktag sign with the words "Help

Keep the Crisis Hotline Hot. Buy a Hotline T-shirt."

"Is my father here yet?" Winnie asked. "He's meeting Karl Fanfield at the airport and then they're coming over here together."

"Not yet," Faith said, "but I don't think Karl Fanfield would arrive this early. It's only four o'clock. The show's not 'til eight."

"I guess you're right," Winnie said, ripping open the carton and unloading stacks of T-shirts in clear plastic bags. "I'm just feeling a little impatient, that's all."

"Don't worry," Faith said. "Everything's going to go smoothly tonight. I can feel it."

"I hope so," Winnie said glumly. "After my fight with Josh last night, I don't need anymore problems. The hotline's depending on it."

"Faith!" called Liza, appearing from behind the red velvet curtains that had been set up in front of the makeshift stage. Her unruly orange curls were pulled up in a top knot that cascaded over the top of her head like a waterfall. Her body overflowed out of hot pink stretch pants and a striped, V-neck sweater.

"Oh boy," Faith said, blowing a strand of blond hair out of her eyes. "All day she's been acting like she's my creative consultant. What does she want now?"

"Give her a chance," Lauren whispered. "She's really not so bad, once you get to know her."

"*Know* her?" Faith said, trying to keep her voice hushed so Liza wouldn't hear. "I *live* with her. What's come over you and KC lately?"

"Yoo hoo! Faith!" Liza called again. "I wanted to talk to you about those lights. You know, I thought it might be more interesting if you tried some colored gels."

Faith rolled her eyes and walked over to Liza. Meanwhile, Winnie sighed as she helped Lauren stack the T-shirts by size. It really did look like the hotline benefit would be a success; everyone on campus was dying to see Karl Fanfield. All 400 tickets had been sold, as well as an additional 100 tickets for standing room. That, plus revenue from the T-shirts, should bring in more than $5,000 for the hotline, enough to really make a difference. Winnie felt very lucky that her father had arranged this for her.

So why was Josh being so negative about Byron all of a sudden? It didn't make sense. Who cared if her father had his credit card rejected? That didn't make him a bad person. And just because Josh was jealous was no reason for Josh to turn her against her father. If Josh were smart, he'd try to learn from Byron. Byron was the most charming person

Winnie had ever met, and she didn't feel that way simply because he was her father.

Why couldn't Josh be more like Byron? Instead, Josh had forced them into another fight, and another break-up. It had taken them months to make up after their last fight. Winnie had been so depressed she'd nearly had a nervous breakdown. She knew she didn't have the strength to go through that again. She didn't think Josh wanted to either. So why did they seem doomed to repeat this vicious cycle of breaking up and making up? Or maybe this time they wouldn't make up again. Maybe this time it was really over.

"Somebody ask for a sound system?" asked a young man in the doorway of Swedenborg House. He wore a tweed sportscoat, wrinkled chinos, and wire-rimmed glasses. Winnie recognized him. It was Meredith, a junior, a drama major, and a friend of Faith's. Behind him, loaded on a dolly, were two large speakers, several miles of black cable, and a portable sound mixing board with little levers on it.

Several pretty young women in pleated skirts, cashmere sweaters, and pearls appeared in the doorway alongside Meredith. They each carried several glossy shopping bags.

"We're from Tri Beta," said a girl whose straight brown hair was pulled back by a powder-pink headband. "I'm Sarah Mills, and this is Marcia Tabbert and Lisa Jean McDermott. We've brought the refreshments. Where should we set up?"

"Winnie!" Faith called from the stage. "I need your opinion! Can you come over here and look at these lights?"

Depressed as Winnie was, it was time to think about something else besides Josh. The show was going to start in a few hours, and there was still a lot of work to do.

"Meredith, we've set up a table back here for your sound board," Winnie said, "and you girls can use that table next to Lauren. I'll check on you in a little while to see if there's anything you need. Coming, Faith!" she yelled, hurrying up toward the stage.

The next few hours were so busy that Winnie was barely aware of the time passing. By quarter to seven, though, Swedenborg House had become an elegant little theater. Liza played stand-in for Karl Fanfield while Faith and Meredith ran a light and sound check.

"Looks good and sounds good," Faith said finally. Now all we need is Karl Fanfield."

"Yeah," Liza said, jumping off the stage with a reverberating thump. "Where is he?"

Winnie looked at her watch. It was ten to seven. Though her father hadn't told her exactly what time Karl's plane was getting in, she'd certainly expected him to arrive by now. The audience would start arriving in less than an hour.

"I hope his plane isn't late," Winnie said. "Maybe my father tried to reach me at the room. I wish I'd thought to give him the number of the pay phone here since Melissa's not there to take a message. That was stupid of me."

"You could call the airline," Lauren suggested. "They can let you know what time the plane arrived."

"I don't know what airline he's flying," Winnie said. "I just left the whole thing up to my father."

"Well, I'll bet your father left you a message at his hotel," Liza said. "Where's he staying?"

"The Springfield Hamptonian. He wrote it on his business card," Winnie said, pulling it out of her pocket and running to the pay phone.

"Don't worry," Faith said, following her. "They're probably stepping out of a taxi as we speak."

"I hope you're right," Winnie said, punching the number into the phone.

"Springfield Hamptonian," said the operator. "May I help you?"

"Yes. My father's staying at your hotel," Winnie said. "I was wondering if he'd left a message for me. Could you check, please? His name is Byron Jennings."

"Certainly," said the operator. "One moment, please." The operator put Winnie on hold, then returned a moment later. "I'm sorry," she said. "But Mr. Jennings is no longer with us. He checked out this morning."

"That can't be!" Winnie said, clutching the cord of the telephone. "I was with him last night and he said he'd be in town until Monday!"

"I'm sorry," the operator said again. "The only information I have is that Mr. Jennings called for a taxi to take him to the airport at nine o'clock this morning."

Winnie hung up the phone with shaking fingers.

"What's going on?" Faith asked, laying a hand on Winnie's shoulder.

"I don't know!" Winnie agonized. "I don't get it. They said he checked out this morning and went to the airport."

"Maybe they just meant he was going to the airport to pick up Karl Fanfield," Faith suggested.

"I don't think so," Winnie said, pacing in a tiny circle. "Karl never would have arrived so early, you said that yourself."

"But your father wouldn't leave town without telling you," Faith said. "And what about Karl Fanfield?"

"I don't know! I don't know!" Winnie repeated, panic-stricken. "I don't know anything anymore.

Maybe my father never really called Karl Fanfield. Maybe he skipped town. Maybe Josh was right about him. Maybe he really is a sleaze."

"Calm down!" Faith said. "Don't over-react. Maybe your father had an emergency this morning and didn't have time to get in touch with you. It might not be what you think."

Winnie checked her watch again. It was now seven o'clock. "All I know is that the show's supposed to start in one hour, and as of right now, we have no entertainment. That's going to do wonders for the hotline budget. Five hundred angry people will be asking for their money back. We've already spent some of the money on T-shirts, which now no one is going to buy because no one's going to stick around once they find out Karl Fanfield's not coming. The hotline's going to end up *owing* money! This is great, this is absolutely great!" Winnie was so angry she kicked the wall.

"You're going too fast," Faith said, pulling two folding chairs over to the phone. "Let's just sit down and try to figure this out calmly."

Winnie allowed Faith to push her gently into the chair.

"Okay," Faith said, taking a pen and a scrap of paper out of the pocket of her jacket. "The first thing we have to do is figure out whether Karl Fanfield's actually coming or not. Since we can't find your father, we'll have to find some other way to track him down. You said Karl's from Denver, right?"

Winnie nodded glumly. "I doubt he's listed in the phone book," she said. "He's too famous."

"I'll call Denver information," Faith said, jumping up and placing a handful of quarters on the metal ledge beneath the phone.

Winnie listened as Faith discovered that Karl Fanfield was indeed not listed. Faith then asked the operator for the names of several comedy clubs in the Denver area. Faith called the first one, Lafftrax and spoke to the manager, who informed her that Karl Fanfield could be reached through his manager, Jennifer Powell. He didn't have the number, but information did. Within seconds, Faith was on the phone with Ms. Powell, explaining the situation.

"I see," Faith said, nodding grimly as she listened. "Uh huh. . . . uh huh. . . . Oh really? Well, I have Byron's daughter here with me. Would you mind telling her what you just told me?" Faith handed Winnie the phone and smiled sympathetically. "I'm here," she whispered. "Just remember that."

"Hello?" Winnie said in an unsteady voice.

"I'm sorry, dear," said a kind-sounding woman. "Your father did call me about getting Karl to perform for your benefit tonight, but he never mentioned that Karl was supposed to appear for free. We were assuming we'd receive a deposit on Karl's fee by this morning, but when it didn't arrive, we had to cancel the engagement. I know this puts you in a terrible position, but there's really nothing I can do about it."

"It's not your fault," Winnie said miserably. "It's my dad's. He really *is* a liar, just like my boyfriend was trying to tell me. I'm just surprised he didn't lie about knowing you."

"Oh, he knows me," the manager said with a small laugh. "And I know him, too. Everybody in Denver knows Byron. He's notorious for making promises he can't keep. He's a flake, a charming flake. Personally, I like him very much. I just wouldn't want to count on him for anything."

"Oh *why* didn't I listen to my mother!" Winnie wailed. "That's what she was trying to tell me all along. If only I'd listened to her in the first place. Now my entire life is ruined!" Winnie began to sob uncontrollably, and Faith took the phone from her hand.

"Thank you, Ms. Powell," she said, hanging it up. Then she hugged Winnie.

Winnie was crying so hard she felt sick to her stomach. Tears poured down her cheeks, onto Faith's T-shirt. But even having Faith there was little comfort. Winnie felt utterly abandoned. First Josh and now her father had disappeared from her life at the very moment she needed their support the most, at the moment she was about to do something really important.

All those months of trying to get to the point where she could be more mature, more responsible, had been wasted. She was right back where she started—with nothing to show for herself. She was a flake and the daughter of a flake. She was genetically doomed to repeat her father's mistakes. All Winnie wanted to do was to run away, to hide, to go back to Jacksonville and give up. It was the only option she had left.

"Excuse me," Liza said, mincing toward her. "I couldn't help overhearing."

Winnie was still crying too hard to answer.

"Don't say a word," Liza said. "I know exactly how you're feeling. Here you are with a show to put on and no star to speak of. What's an impresario to do? But I think I have a solution to your problem."

Fourteen

"I've gone down the Wahalla River half a dozen times," Brooks said. He was telling the story for the fourteenth time. "But this was the first time I did it on my rear end. I don't think I'll be able to sit down for a week." His damp curls clung to his head, goosebumps dotted his arms, and his wet T-shirt fit him like a second skin.

Melissa, freezing cold and soaking wet, stood next to Brooks on the rocky riverbank counting her bruises. She had a dozen purple splotches on each leg, several more on each arm, and she, too, planned to stand up on the ride home.

At least she still *could* stand up. When Melissa had first jumped in with the crazy idea that she

_181_

could save Brooks, she'd been dragged down beneath the water by a suck hole. She'd felt utterly helpless as she swirled around and around, her powerful athlete's body no match for the force of nature. All she'd been able to do was hold her breath and hope the water would fling her back up to the surface before she blacked out.

Melissa had popped up a few seconds later, and she'd searched frantically for Brooks, trying at the same time to avoid the pointed rocks coming at her on both sides. She'd seen a small white helmet way ahead of her, bobbing as it was carried along by the crashing waves. What could she have been thinking of when she jumped in? She couldn't save him. She couldn't even reach him.

Melissa had tried to relax and keep her feet straight ahead of her as Susan, their guide had instructed, but the water kept turning her from side to side, and she kept banging into rocks. Eventually, she'd become so cold that it had numbed the pain, and she'd found she could steer a bit by angling her body to one side or the other. At last she'd arrived in the calmer water with all her limbs still attached to her body.

Susan, Josh, and Phoenix had fished them into the raft, and the two had lain in the bottom of the boat like pieces of soggy seaweed. They hadn't said a word to each other as Susan and the others paddled to shore. Now as they stood on the rocks, waiting for the bus to pick them up, Melissa felt the silence like a dead weight. There was so much they needed to say to each other. Melissa had to begin somewhere, anywhere.

"You still cold?" she asked.

Brooks shrugged. "Nothing a few days in a pizza oven wouldn't cure."

Melissa laughed through chattering teeth. "I'm glad you're okay."

"You shouldn't have jumped in after me," Brooks said. His eyes were worried, but his voice was warm. "Do you realize how foolish that was? If something had happened to you, I never could have forgiven myself."

"What about me?" Melissa demanded. "How do you think *I* would have felt if you'd drowned and I hadn't done everything I could to save you?"

Brooks smiled. "I guess that means you still care about me. You know, I had a lot of time to think as I was floating down the Wahalla. I kept thinking that if I died today, my one regret would be that I pushed things too fast. It was stupid of me to ask you to marry me. I had no right to make it seem like an ultimatum."

"You had every right." Melissa moved closer to Brooks and clasped her arms around his shoulders. Cold as they both were, a warmth traveled between their bodies. Melissa tilted her head up so she could look in Brooks's eyes. "You can ask me anything you want," she said softly. "It's up to me to say yes or no. I did some thinking, too, as I was floating along. I was so worried that something would happen to you. I kept trying to imagine life without you, and I just couldn't. It made me realize how much I love you. I don't think I could ever stand being apart from you."

"Thank you," Brooks said, closing his eyes and squeezing Melissa tightly. "You don't know how much it means to me to hear you say that."

"No, no," Melissa said in an urgent tone that made Brooks open his eyes again. "You don't understand. What I'm saying is—I've thought about your marriage proposal. And my answer is yes."

At seven o'clock, Peter sat with KC in the nearly-empty dining commons. He tilted back in his chair, a satisfied, almost maternal grin on his face.

"What are you looking at?" KC asked, wiping her lips with a paper napkin. Her cheeks had lost that drawn, sunken look and her smooth skin had a healthy glow.

Peter looked from KC to her empty plates, all five of them. She'd devoured half a chicken, a side order of green beans and rice, two buttered rolls, three graham crackers with peanut butter, and half a dozen chocolate chip cookies. "Had enough?" he joked. "I guess I won't have to bring you any more doggie bags from the cafeteria."

Anxiety flitted across KC's large, gray eyes, but it was replaced by defiance. "I'm just trying to gain back the weight I lost," she said. "After that, it's back to my usual routine. Don't worry, I'm not letting myself go."

Peter laughed. "Worried is hardly the word I'd use to express how I feel about you right now." He checked his watch. "It's seven o'clock," he said. "I guess we should start heading over to Swedenborg House. Didn't you say you wanted to help Winnie?"

"I was at Tri Beta all day overseeing the refreshments," KC said, "and she seemed to have everything under control last night when we saw her, so we can take our time. Besides, there's something I wanted to discuss with you before we go." KC clasped her hands on the table as if she were about to chair a business meeting.

"Uh oh," Peter said. "Sounds very official. What is it?"

KC cleared her throat. "Um . . . yes. This is very difficult for me to say."

Peter grew instantly wary. Had he been so relaxed, so comfortable with KC lately that he'd missed some warning sign? Her face, her tone, her words—was she about to tell him something he didn't want to hear? Peter tilted forward in his chair and grabbed the edge of the table for support. "Go ahead," he said, bracing himself.

"I'm a very independent person, as you know . . ." KC began, looking down at the empty plates stacked on her tray.

Uh oh. This was even worse than he thought. The axe was about to fall on Peter's unsuspecting neck and there was absolutely nothing he could do about it.

". . . or at least I've tried to be," KC said. "All my life I've done everything on my own—not counting on my friends or family."

"Let me save you the trouble," Peter said, willing his face to show none of the terror that was gripping his heart. "What you're trying to say is . . ."

"Let me finish," KC said. "You don't know what I'm about to say. I'm trying to tell you that I realized something about myself at my modeling shoot the other day. Something important. I'm not a superwoman or an automaton. I've always thought I didn't need to depend on anyone, but I was wrong. I'm human. And sometimes I can't make it on my own. Sometimes I need other people to help me. Oh, I'm not saying this right."

Peter felt his grip on the table loosen and he

started to breathe again. "Keep trying," he encouraged her.

KC huffed out a short, frustrated sigh. "I'm so bad at talking about my emotions," she said. "You'll have to forgive me. What I'm really trying to say is —I don't just need people. I need *you*. I've been a real jerk for trying to act like it was any different. A stupid, defensive jerk. I need you. There. I've said it twice. And I mean it. I hope it's not too late to tell you this."

"Too late?" Peter practically shouted, leaping up and kissing KC across the table. "Do you know how long I've waited to hear those words? I would have waited another year if I'd known you'd say it in the end."

This was turning out to be the best day of Peter's life! When he'd first laid eyes on KC, he'd never dreamed that someone as beautiful as she would talk to him, let alone admit she needed or loved him. Peter sat back down in a daze. He wasn't sure his body could hold so much happiness.

KC looked down shyly at her still-folded hands. "I hope you'll still wait around for another year, even though there's no prize at the end of it except me still loving you. I hope you'll wait around for a lot more years."

Peter felt a stabbing sensation in his chest at KC's words. With all the tension he'd been feeling, then the overwhelming joy, he'd nearly forgotten about the conversation he'd had on the phone this morning. The conversation that could throw everything up in the air again.

KC smiled at Peter with such sweetness, with an openness and vulnerability he'd never seen in her before. How could he tell her that he'd just learned he'd made the finals again for the Morgan Foundation Photo Contest? How could he tell her that if he won, he'd be offered a scholarship to study in Europe for a year, which meant they wouldn't have much more time together? KC would be devastated. She'd never open up to him again.

Then again, even if Peter *did* win, he wasn't sure he'd take the scholarship. Important as it was to his career, he didn't feel he could *ever* leave KC. Not for this, not for anything.

Fifteen

....

It was 7:55 p.m. Winnie wanted to throw her watch to the floor and stomp on it until it was just a heap of cogs and springs. That seemed like the only way to stop time from moving forward—to the moment when 500 people would be clamoring around her, angrily demanding their money back. Most of them had already taken their seats and were chattering happily. Their faces showed how eager they were to see Karl Fanfield, major celebrity, right here on campus.

Winnie stood alone on the darkened, empty stage, peering through a crack in the red velvet curtains at the soon-to-be-disappointed audience. People were still pouring through the door, finding their seats, but there was no sign of Liza or Faith.

When Liza had heard the bad news about Karl Fanfield, she'd suggested that she and Faith round up some of the performing arts students from Coleridge Hall as replacement entertainers. Winnie had turned Liza down at first, arguing that now no one would settle for amateurs when they'd paid for a Hollywood comedian with an HBO special and his own NBC sitcom.

Liza had talked her into it, though, arguing that even a slapped-together show was better than nothing. Faith, to her own surprise, had agreed with Liza, saying that no show meant no money for the hotline. At least if they tried to put something together at the last minute, there was a chance some people wouldn't ask for their money back.

Since she had no other choice, Winnie had agreed. That was nearly an hour ago, but there was still no sign of Faith or Liza or anyone else who could save her. There probably hadn't been anyone around in Coleridge when they went to look. If only she hadn't changed her mind about using student performers. Now they were probably all out enjoying the weekend. Some might even have bought tickets to the benefit.

Winnie had to face it. In a few minutes, she'd have to go out there, alone, in front of the audience and explain that the show was canceled. Winnie just hoped that no one in the audience happened to be carrying any rotten tomatoes.

"Winnie!" said Teresa Gray, stepping up to the stage from the rear. She was dressed in a tuxedo jacket, dress shirt, bow tie, and blue jeans. David Arthur was behind her, dressed in a hotline T-shirt and corduroy pants. Both of them wore worried expressions. David kept running a hand through his thinning hair. Winnie hoped they weren't carrying any tomatoes either.

"Uh, hi," Winnie said sheepishly. "I guess you're wondering what's going on here."

"We already heard," Teresa said with concern. "Have you told the audience yet?"

"Not yet," Winnie said. "I'm still waiting for some of my theatrical friends to show up and bail us out. We figured a show with U. of S. students was better than no show."

Teresa nodded glumly. David kept running his fingers through his hair; no wonder it was falling out. But he had every right to be mad. They both did. They'd put their confidence and trust in her and she'd let them down.

"I can't tell you how sorry I am," Winnie said, clutching the velvet curtains for support.

"I'm sure it wasn't your fault," Teresa said.

"It was and it wasn't," Winnie said. "The mistake

I made was trusting a father I hadn't seen in sixteen years. I should have realized that sixteen years of neglect means something, no matter how convincing his excuses were. But that's not your problem. I mean, you get enough of that every time you answer the phone at the hotline. The real problem is —what do we do now? Like I said, I've got some friends working on it, not that any of them is Karl Fanfield, although Faith said there's this guy in her dorm who sort of *looks* like Karl Fanfield. Liza said maybe they could dim the lights and try to fool people and. . . ."

Winnie realized that she was babbling and that Teresa and David were looking at her a bit puzzled. They were probably wondering why they'd ever agreed to let her answer phones, let alone organize the benefit. Thanks to her, the hotline would be even more broke than it was before they'd started. Maybe it would even have to close! Winnie felt a pain in her stomach when she thought about all the desperate callers who might never get the help they needed, thanks to her.

"It's a quarter after eight," Teresa said. "I don't think we should keep them waiting any longer. It will just make them angrier when they find out Fanfield's not here."

"I agree," said David. "One of us has to go out there."

"I'll do it," Winnie said. "I got us into this mess. I should be the one who has to face them."

"Good luck," Teresa said tonelessly, walking away from Winnie in the darkness. David followed.

It was time. Winnie closed her eyes and imagined the cheerful, laughing faces turning into an angry mob. She pictured their grasping, clutching fingers, as they demanded their money back. It was like a scene in a horror movie.

Winnie forced herself to part the curtains and step out onto the front lip of the stage. The spotlights were blinding, and for a moment, Winnie had to shield her eyes with her hands. The murmuring crowd fell into an expectant hush and Winnie could feel the 500 eager faces turned up toward her.

"Ladies and gentlemen," she began in a croaky voice.

"Can't hear you!" someone called good-naturedly from the audience.

"Use the microphone!" someone else directed her.

Winnie stumbled toward the free-standing microphone at the very front of the stage, the one Karl Fanfield was supposed to have used. "I'd like to thank you for coming and showing your support for the Crisis Hotline," she began, but microphone feedback screeched from the speakers above her head, drowning her out. "As you know, the hotline helps or refers hundreds of people in our area with all kinds of problems like drug addiction, alcoholism, depression—people who feel they have nowhere else to turn." Winnie knew she was delaying the inevitable. She was also making a play for their sympathy, hoping that would lessen their anger, but she couldn't keep this up much longer. She had to tell them the truth.

"I know you were expecting Karl Fanfield," Winnie started to say, but she was interrupted by a loud crash as the doors to Swedenborg House flew open and Liza appeared, bursting out of a tight, orange unitard which she wore with her silver lamé cowboy boots. She strode straight up the center aisle of the makeshift theater, leading a ragtag bunch of students from Coleridge Hall.

Faith was right behind Liza, carrying a guitar case and a clown costume. Dante Borelli, a theater major, was dressed in a straw boater hat and an old-fashioned suit with a bow tie. Winnie recognized it as the costume he'd worn when he'd performed "Trouble in River City" at the U. of S. Follies a few weeks ago. A group of athletic-looking girls in revealing, colorful, Lycra midriff tops and bicycle shorts followed, eliciting whistles from several of the men in the audience. Winnie lost track after that. She saw Freya, Faith's opera-singing neighbor.

She saw hands toting tap shoes, makeup cases, and powdered wigs.

Winnie was too startled to say anything, but she didn't have to. Liza jumped up onto the stage, waved the others around to the back, and grabbed the microphone from Winnie. "I'll take over from here," she whispered, giving Winnie a big, theatrical wink. Winnie noticed that Liza was wearing false eyelashes.

"Thanks!" Winnie whispered before backing gratefully through the curtain. She jumped off the side of the stage and saw that Faith and the others had already set up a make-shift dressing room. They were painting their faces, changing into costumes, pulling instruments out of cases and tuning them. Winnie rushed around to the front so she could see what Liza would do.

Liza glowed orange in the spotlight, from her long, curly hair to her over-abundant body, bulging out of the shiny, form-fitting bodysuit. Her red lips looked like a valentine in the middle of her pale, white face, and her shiny boots glinted as she strutted over to the microphone and grabbed it.

"As you can see," she said in a comical, sultry voice, "I am *not* Karl Fanfield." There were some boos in the audience, but there were also some catcalls and whoops. *Probably guys who liked her tight costume,* Winnie thought. "But what's Karl Fanfield got that I ain't got?" she asked, jutting out one ample hip as a drummer behind Winnie beat out a tattoo.

"You got a lot more than Karl Fanfield!" one guy shouted from the audience.

Liza grinned. "Okay," she said confidently. "Here's the bad news. Karl Fanfield couldn't make it. A serious, *deathly* illness. Who knows? We might not ever see him on NBC next year."

Winnie was amazed at Liza's gall, lying like that in front of all those people. She was worried, too, at the angry mutterings she heard from the audience. Any second now, people were going to start getting up and walking out.

"But," Liza said, shooting one red-nailed finger up in the air, "before you start getting all upset over nothing, I'd like to make you an offer. We have a show for you tonight. A show never before seen anywhere on the planet, and never to be seen again after tonight. A show featuring the up-and-coming stars of tomorrow, not some shlocky comedian you can see on reruns of the Carson show. We've got song, we've got dance, and most of all, we've got *me!*"

"Woo!" someone screamed from the other side of the room.

"You know me. You love me. I stole your hearts when I sang for you at the Springfield Follies," Liza said, flouncing over to the side of the stage where Faith handed her a guitar and a cowboy hat. "So here's the deal. You stay right where you are until intermission. If you're not having a good time, and I know you will, we'll give you your money back. Now I'd like to sing you a song that I learned as a little girl, growing up in the backwoods of Brooklyn, New York."

Winnie listened as Liza sang an outrageous parody of a country and western song, followed by a five-minute comic monologue about how it felt to be a pushy New Yorker in a state where people were too polite to tell you you're stepping on their toe. After Liza, Dante reprised his number from *The Music Man*, "Trouble in River City," followed by two mimes who skillfully simulated being stuck in an elevator in an earthquake and plunging forty flights without the use of props or special effects. A clown juggled while tap dancing on roller skates. Finally, Meredith plugged in a tape of rap music, and the girls in bicycle shorts did an athletic, funky, synchronized dance that had the audience clapping and cheering as the house lights came up.

It was intermission. Time to see how many people wanted their money back. With Peter's help, Winnie had moved the T-shirt table near the entrance and had lettered another sign which read, simply, Refunds. Winnie waited nervously as several people approached them, but all they asked was how much the T-shirts cost. Then they each bought one.

By the time intermission was over, Winnie wanted to cheer, too. Only five people had asked for their money back! That meant the hotline could renovate the offices and stay in business.

Faith, who'd stood by Winnie and Peter as they waited, hugged Winnie hard and spun her around. "We did it!" she squealed. "We really did it!"

"I can't thank you enough," Winnie said. "You guys saved my life. You may even have saved some other people's lives for real—the people who call in to the hotline."

"I was glad to help," Faith said. "But I'm not the one you should be thanking." Faith glanced back toward the audience where Liza was working the crowd, flirting, joking, shaking hands. Liza seemed to be trying, single-handedly, to charm people into staying.

"She's pretty amazing, isn't she?" Winnie said.

Faith nodded slowly. "I never thought I would say this," she said, "but I think I'm actually beginning to like her."

Sixteen

· ·

"**G**ood evening, miss," said the maitre d'
in a low, sexy voice. "May I show you
to your table?"

Lauren entered Dash's rented room, lit only by
two flickering candles that cast huge, dancing shad-
ows on the wall. The candles stood on his kitchen
table, which was really just an oak door balanced on
stacks of cinder blocks. The table was covered with
a white sheet and set with two mismatched plates,
plastic champagne glasses, and silverware that might
have been "borrowed" from the diner across the
street. The air was filled with the warm, steamy
smell of chicken cooking, and there was a loaf of

fresh bread in a basket on the kitchen's beige Formica counter.

Dash, playing maitre d', wore a white dinner jacket over his T-shirt, and a plaid dishtowel over his arm. His smooth skin glowed in the candlelight, and his dark eyes smoldered as he looked down at her. Lauren blushed, not from embarrassment, but at how handsome he was. No matter how many times she looked at him, she felt the same mixture of excitement and desire as the first night they'd kissed.

"I've heard so much about this restaurant," Lauren said softly, playing along. "I was lucky to get a reservation."

Dash took her arm and guided her to the table, where he pulled out the folding chair for her to sit down.

"Such service!" Lauren said, smiling. "I'll have to remember to give the staff a big tip when dinner is over."

"That's what we're counting on," Dash said, taking the plates off the table and bringing them to the stove. When he turned around, the plates were loaded with wild rice, pencil-thin asparagus, and chicken in a fragrant sauce with capers and olives.

"Dash!" Lauren exclaimed. "This is beautiful! You're a real chef."

Dash shrugged as he sat down across from

Lauren. "If the journalism thing doesn't work out for me, maybe I can get a job slinging hash in a diner."

"More like some four-star restaurant," Lauren commented as Dash poured them each a glass of champagne.

Dash raised his glass between the candles, and Lauren lifted hers to meet it. "To us," he said as their glasses touched.

"To your health," Lauren added. "And here's to our spending a lot more time together, now that you're well."

Lauren and Dash sipped their champagne and smiled at each other over their glasses.

"We've got a lot to catch up on," Dash said. "I haven't really spoken to you in weeks. Tell me what you've been doing. Have you written any more stories for the paper? Greg said you've been making yourself kind of scarce around the *Journal* office lately."

Lauren sighed as she unfolded her paper napkin and placed it on her lap. "I have been working on something," she admitted, "but I didn't want Greg to know about it until it was finished. At the rate I'm going, though, it may never be finished."

"What is it?" Dash asked, eating a forkful of chicken.

"Promise not to tell, okay? I've been trying to

cover the men's volleyball team. I thought it would stretch my range as a reporter. I even had the nerve to go into the men's locker room, thanks to Liza Ruff. I was in the middle of some really good interviews when the coach kicked us out. So I barely got a page of notes. Hardly enough to write a story."

Dash looked down at his plate and became very busy cutting up his chicken breast. "That's too bad," he mumbled.

"But I'm not backing down," Lauren continued. "In fact, this whole ordeal gave me an idea for an even *better* story. You know, they have a reception area for women athletes to talk to male reporters, but the only way to cover men's sporting events is to go into the locker room. And if male reporters are allowed in, female reporters should be allowed, too. If they're kept out, that's discriminatory and sexist. I'm planning to write an exposé on it for the *Journal*. I was thinking of calling it 'Out of the Locker Room: Women Reporters Who Won't Throw in the Towel.'"

Dash, who'd just eaten a mouthful of rice, started to choke.

"Dash!" Lauren exclaimed, jumping up and coming around the table to see if she could help him. "Are you okay?"

Dash stood up and ran to the sink, where he filled up a glass with water. It took him several gulps before he could talk again. "I'm fine," he said, sitting down again. "It's just that your story is sort of related to the one Greg just assigned me."

"Really?" Lauren asked. "What a coincidence! Maybe we could work on it together."

"I don't think so," Dash said, taking another sip of water. "We're sort of on opposite sides of the issue."

"What do you mean?"

"Well, uh, the reason Greg called me in this morning was because he heard that the volleyball coach was complaining about two unnamed females harrassing his players."

"Uh oh . . ." Lauren said, taking another sip of champagne.

"Greg thought we should do an article on reverse discrimination. Coach Brandes was outraged that female reporters could just barge into the men's locker room while a male reporter could never enter a women's locker room. There's definitely a double standard here. And my assignment is to argue why *men* should be allowed to go into the *women's* locker room!"

The cheers and applause had faded to echoes in Winnie's mind as she folded the last of the chairs in Swedenborg House. The stage had been dismantled, the sound system carted away, and everyone else had gone home. Winnie had remained behind, though, just to feel the peace and silence in the empty room.

It was all over now, and Winnie felt a tiredness permeating her entire body. It would feel good to get some sleep after all the trauma and excitement. Winnie knew she'd sleep well. The benefit had pulled in $5,540, more than enough to repaint and refurnish the hotline office, buy a new sign, and extend the janitor's hours so they could stay open longer. There was even enough left over to buy a coffee pot and refrigerator so the hotline volunteers could have some refreshment while they were working.

Teresa and David had been ecstatic when they'd left, thanking Winnie over and over. She'd saved the hotline, they said. They'd been wrong for doubting she could pull it off. She was a hero.

Liza, too, had been treated like a superstar. Everyone from Coleridge wanted to shake her hand, and some of her fans asked for her autograph, just in case she really did turn out to be famous one day. A film student even wanted to do a documentary about her life! KC and Faith had whisked her away at the end, though, with Faith offering to treat to a midnight sub at Hondo's Cafe. They'd wanted Winnie to come too, but Winnie preferred to be by herself right now.

Taking one last look around Swedenborg House to make sure everything was in order, Winnie turned off the chandeliers and locked the door. She took her time walking across the green toward her dorm. It had been a warm day, and the evening air coming down off the mountains was pleasantly cool and fresh. Crickets chirped in throbbing harmony.

Winnie smiled to herself as she headed down the grassy slope toward Forest Hall. It was funny, but even though her life was in shambles, she felt perfectly calm inside. After all, what more could go wrong? She'd opened up to her father, trusted him, only to learn that he was a liar and a fake. She'd lost Josh again; there was no way their relationship could survive another long separation like the one they'd had last time. She'd almost faced the biggest screw-up of her life when Karl Fanfield didn't show up for the benefit.

But that, in a way, was the reason Winnie didn't feel so terrible. When the worst had happened, she hadn't run away like she might have done before. She'd been scared, but she'd gone out there to face the audience. That was progress for Winnie—real progress. It meant that even if Winnie had to be alone for the rest of her life, at least she could count on herself.

Winnie pushed open the door to Forest Hall. For once, it was quiet, probably because the jock fraternity was having a big beer bash tonight, which meant everyone in her dorm was probably passed out somewhere along Greek Row. Winnie cut through the lobby, her running shoes squeaking against the linoleum, and trudged up the stairs to her floor.

The second floor, too, was quiet. Without meaning to, Winnie felt herself slow down as she neared Josh's room. What was she hoping for, anyway? Hadn't she just told herself that she could face being alone? Winnie forced herself to walk faster, but then heard a slight creak behind her. Winnie turned and saw Josh's door had opened a crack. An eye peered at her from the dark. Then the door closed abruptly.

Josh? Winnie wanted to call out, despite herself. But Josh wouldn't have heard her. His door was closed. And he couldn't have wanted to see her that badly, or he would have come out to talk to her.

Winnie pulled her key out of her pocket and unlocked the door to her room. Bed. Sleep. That was the only thing left to her now. Winnie started to close the door, but she couldn't quite get herself to shut it all the way. She peered out through the crack in her door, back down the hall, and saw that Josh's door had opened again. Their eyes met. Winnie almost laughed at how silly this was. Josh must have been thinking the same thing, because he waved sheepishly and came out into the hall. Winnie, too, opened her door and moved slowly down the hall toward him. Josh met her halfway, and they stood for a moment, staring at each other silently.

Josh's brown hair was rumpled and he wore a wrinkled T-shirt that said Computerland—All your software needs and more! His long, thin legs poked out of baggy shorts, and his heels crushed the backs of his worn leather moccasins.

"How was the benefit?" Josh asked, his voice level. "Did Karl Fanfield show up?"

Winnie shook her head.

"I'm sorry," Josh said. "I tried to warn you."

"I know," Winnie said. "I guess you were right. But this never would have happened in the first place if you hadn't been so keen on getting me back together with my father. Why couldn't you just let me ignore him like I wanted to?"

"I know," Josh said. "I shouldn't have interfered. It was none of my business. I just didn't want you to miss out on something that could have made you happy. I should have checked him out first, though, before putting you through that."

Winnie shrugged. "How could you have known? He's an expert at fooling people. Even *I* was fooled. It's not your fault he's the way he is."

Josh gave Winnie a small smile. "I'm glad you finally realize that."

Winnie smiled too, embarrassed. "I guess that's what I was doing, right? Blaming you."

Josh nodded. "Uh huh."

"I'm sorry," Winnie said. They stood again in silence. Winnie didn't want to leave, but she didn't know what else to say.

"Have you seen Melissa since she got back from the rafting trip?" Josh asked.

Winnie shook her head. "Why?"

"You're never going to believe it," Josh said. "Brooks asked her to marry him and she said yes!"

"You're kidding!" Winnie shrieked. "She said yes?! But they're so young!"

"I know." Josh grinned. "This has been a crazy day."

"Not just today," Winnie said. "This year. My whole life."

"Tell me about it," Josh said. "When I think about how much has happened since we started college, to you, me, to you and me, and all our friends, I could get a real headache." He sat down on the floor and leaned against the cinderblock wall.

Winnie sat down beside him. "So many fights, break-ups, misunderstandings . . ."

"I guess that's what life is all about," Josh said. "Not that there aren't plenty of good things too, but maybe that's what we're *really* supposed to learn in college. I'll bet years from now, when we look back, we're not going to remember which classes we took or the papers we wrote. We're going to remember the people, the relationships . . ."

"Even the ones that ended?" Winnie asked anxiously, trying to hold back the tears. For some reason, sitting here so close to Josh, it was getting harder and harder to face the thought of living without him.

Josh turned to Winnie and put his arm around her shoulder. "Listen to me," he said. "Just because we had a fight doesn't mean we have to break up. It's unrealistic for us to think we're going to agree with each other all the time. The important thing is to keep going. We can yell at each other, insult each other, fight with each other, but that doesn't mean we don't both still care about each other."

"Or love each other," Winnie added softly, feeling a tear trickle out of the corner of her eye.

"Or love each other," Josh echoed, pulling Winnie closer. "We just have to agree that no matter what happens, we'll stay together. We mean too much to one another not to."

"Much too much," Winnie whispered. The last thing she saw before she closed her eyes was Josh's tender face, leaning forward to cover her lips with his own.

Be sure to look for Freshman Flames, the thirteenth book in the dramatic story of FRESHMAN DORM, coming in October.

Coming in September
from HarperPaperbacks:

The Vampire Diaries
A Trilogy
Volume I: The Awakening

Meet Stefan and Damon Salvatore, five-hundred-year old vampire brothers locked in eternal combat . . . Meet Elena Gilbert, the beautiful twentieth century young woman they both love . . . Join Stefan, Damon, and Elena as they are drawn into a passionate love triangle that can only end in horror and despair. . . .

Here's an excerpt from Volume 1, *The Awakening*:

Two lost souls . . .

September 26
Dear Diary,

I'm sorry it's been so long, and I can't really explain why I haven't written—except that there are so many things I feel frightened to talk about, even to you.

First, the most terrible thing happened. The day that Bonnie and Meredith and I were at the cemetery, an old man was attacked there, and almost killed. The police still haven't found the person who did it. People think the old man was crazy because when he woke up he started raving about "eyes in the dark" and oak trees and things. But I remember what happened to <u>us</u> that night, and I wonder. It scares me.

Everyone was scared for a while, and all the kids had to stay inside after dark or go out in groups. But it's been about three weeks now, and no more attacks, so the excitement is dying down. Aunt Judith says it must have been another vagrant that did it. Tyler Smallwood's father even suggested that the old man might have done it to himself—although I would like to see somebody bite himself in the throat.

But I don't really care about the attack. There's only one thing I do care about right now. Stefan.

Even Bonnie and Meredith don't realize how important he is to me. I'm afraid to tell them; I'm afraid they'll think I'm crazy. At school I wear a mask of calm and control, but on the inside—well, every day it just gets worse.

Aunt Judith has started to worry about me. She says I don't eat enough these days, and she's right. I can't seem to concentrate on my classes, or even on anything fun like the Haunted House fundraiser. I can't concentrate on anything but him. And I don't even understand why.

He hasn't spoken to me since that horrible afternoon when he snubbed me in front of everyone. But I'll tell you something strange. Last week in history class I glanced up and caught him looking at me. We were sitting a few seats apart, and he was turned completely sideways in his desk, just looking. For a moment I felt almost frightened, and my heart started pounding, and we just stared at each other—and then he looked away. But since then it's happened twice more, and each time I felt his eyes on me before I saw them. This is the literal truth. I know it's not my imagination.

Every day it's getting worse for me. I feel as if I were a clock or something, winding up tighter and tighter. If I don't find something to do soon, I'll—

I was going to say "die."

Memory engulfed Stefan. It was bad enough when Elena was out of sight, when the cool glow of her mind only teased at the edges of his consciousness. But to be in the same room with her at the school, to feel her presence behind him, to smell the heady fragrance of her skin all around him, was almost more than he could bear.

He had heard every soft breath she took, felt her warmth radiating against his back, sensed each throb of her sweet pulse. And eventually, to his horror, he had found himself giving in to it. His tongue had brushed back and forth over his canine teeth, enjoying the pleasure-pain that was building there, encouraging it. He'd breathed her smell into his nostrils deliberately, and let the visions come to him, imagining it all. How soft her neck would be, and how his lips would meet it with equal softness at first, planting tiny kisses here, and here, until he reached the yielding hollow of her throat. How he would nuzzle there, in the place where her heart beat so strongly against the delicate skin. And how at last his lips would part, would draw back from aching teeth now sharp as little daggers, and—

No. He'd brought himself out of the trance with a jerk, his own pulse beating raggedly, his body shaking. The class had been dismissed, movement was all around him, and he could only hope no one had been observing him too closely.

And then when she had spoken to him, he had been unable to believe that he had to face her while his veins burned and his whole upper jaw ached. He'd been afraid for a moment that his control would break, that he would seize her shoulders and take her in front of all of them. He had no idea how he'd gotten away.